PETTICOAT WAGON TRAIN

**Center Point
Large Print**

**This Large Print Book carries the
Seal of Approval of N.A.V.H.**

PETTICOAT WAGON TRAIN

WAYNE C. LEE

CENTER POINT PUBLISHING

THORNDIKE, MAINE

This Center Point Large Print edition
is published in the year 2004 by arrangement with
Golden West Literary Agency.

The text of this Large Print edition is unabridged. In other
aspects, this book may vary from the original edition. Printed in
Thailand. Set in 16-point Times New Roman type.

ISBN 1-58547-452-5

Library of Congress Cataloging-in-Publication Data

Lee, Wayne C.
    Petticoat wagon train / Wayne C. Lee.--Center Point large print ed.
        p. cm.
    ISBN 1-58547-452-5 (lib. bdg. : alk. paper)
    1. Wagon trains--Fiction. 2. Women pioneers--Fiction. 3. Large type books. I. Title.

PS3523.E34457P48 2004
813'.54--dc22

                                                                    2004000965

I

Jeff Ryan saw the rider coming. Checking his gun, he moved over behind his picketed horse. That was one of the disadvantages of camping out on the open prairie; there was no place to hide.

The rider didn't look like Ross Grilli; he wasn't big enough. Anyway, Grilli was supposed to be in Colorado. That was why Jeff was heading that way in the next day or two.

The rider came straight toward Jeff's camp and didn't appear unfriendly. But Jeff kept his hand on his gun. He was too wise in the ways of the prairie to take any chances.

The rider reined up ten yards from Jeff. "Howdy. Are you Jefferson Ryan?"

Jeff studied the stranger, who was little more than a fuzzy-cheeked kid; he wasn't even carrying a gun. Jeff's alarm faded but his vigilance remained.

"I'm Jeff Ryan," he said. "Why are you interested?"

"I've got a message for you." He swung down without an invitation.

He either lacked range etiquette or had a sinister purpose in dismounting without being invited. Jeff remained alert.

"Who sent you?" he demanded.

"Mr. Beanigan."

Jeff frowned. "You mean Beany Beanigan?"

The boy nodded. "I reckon that's what most folks

call him. My name is Norrie Fergison. Mr. Beanigan just hired me. He wants to see you at the Longhorn Restaurant in town."

"What for?" Jeff asked suspiciously.

He circled the idea like a wary coyote. Beany Beanigan was Abe Ryan's right hand man. He was supposed to be on Abe's ranch in Colorado, not here on the outskirts of Kansas City.

"Mr. Beanigan didn't tell me why he wanted to see you. He just said to tell you he'd meet you at the Longhorn at ten o'clock."

"And he expects me to come running just like that?" Jeff said.

"I reckon," Norrie said. "He didn't appear to doubt that you'd come."

"The old goat's right," Jeff said. "Tell him I'll be there. And he'd better have something to tell me that's worth the trip."

"I reckon he has," Norrie said, and swung back into the saddle.

He spurred his horse back toward the town on the big river as if he was afraid Jeff would ask more questions. Jeff would have liked some answers but this kid wasn't going to give him any. If he knew anything, Beany had apparently warned him not to tell.

If Beany had a message for Jeff, it must be from his Uncle Abe. But why hadn't Beany ridden out here himself? He must know where Jeff was camped or he couldn't have sent Norrie Fergison here.

It lacked half an hour of being ten o'clock when Jeff

reined up at the hitchrack in front of the Longhorn Restaurant. Looking through the big front window, he saw Beany at the table just inside. Beany was early, too. He must be anxious to see him. Or else this was a trap with Beany as the bait.

Jeff tied his horse and crossed the walk to the door. Stepping inside, he scanned the almost empty room. Nothing seemed amiss. He turned to the table where Beany waited with a cup of coffee. Dropping into a chair, he faced the short, rather heavy-set, bowlegged man and stuck out a hand.

"Good to see you, Beany. Now tell me what the ruckus is."

Beany shook Jeff's hand. "Sure good to see you, Jeff. Been a while. Who said there was a ruckus?"

"You didn't send that kid out there just to invite me in here for a dinner," Jeff said.

"You're right." Beany agreed. "All you get is a cup of coffee." He waved to the girl behind the counter and held up a finger.

"What are you doing here on the river?" Jeff demanded.

"Abe sent me," Beany said. "I brought three wagons, supplies, six horses to pull the wagons, and three extra saddle horses. Hired my drivers. All I got left to do is sign you on to boss the wagon train."

Jeff stared at Beany as if he'd lost his mind. Jeff had spent the last eight years guiding wagon trains to Oregon and California. But with the completion of the railroad to the west coast, the only travelers going over the plains in wagons now were those who couldn't afford to rent an emigrant car on the railroad.

"A three-wagon train?" he asked incredulously. "What's in those wagons?"

"Supplies for the ranch," Beany said.

The girl brought the cup of coffee for Jeff. "It ain't that far to Colorado," Jeff said. "Or that dangerous any more. Why don't you do the job yourself?"

"Mainly because Abe sent me to get you. He got a fall from a horse not long ago. He needs help, Jeff, and he's always said you'd be the one who would come if he needed help."

Jeff nodded, frowning. "Uncle Abe and Aunt Miranda practically raised me after my folks died. But I'm fiddle-footed."

"Abe knows that. Says it's time you settled down. You'll be too old to get a start if you don't do it pretty soon."

Jeff knew Abe was right. He was twenty-eight. He'd been on the trail for eleven years, eight of them as a guide and wagon boss.

"Abe needs you, Jeff," Beany added. "He told me to tell you that he's aiming to cut you in as a partner on the AR if you come."

Jeff's eyes widened. "Partner? Uncle Abe don't need a partner."

"He does now. He ain't going to be able to run that ranch much longer. He was too old when he moved out there. He figures you'll run it before long—his ranch, your work—equal shares. How does that sound?"

Jeff nodded, knowing that he didn't dare pass up this

opportunity. "Good," he said. "But I've got a job to do first. I had a partner named Ross Grilli who worked with me on trains where I was wagon boss. We quarreled—doesn't matter what about. He's a vindictive fellow, I found out. He swore he'd get even with me for the licking I gave him. He stole my horse and what little money I had. I'm flat busted. I figure I owe him something now."

"If you're busted," Beany said quickly, "you need this job."

"You sold me," Jeff said, grinning. "Mainly because I heard just yesterday that Grilli is in Colorado, has been there for a while. So I'm going there, anyway." He studied Beany's face. "Why didn't you have me meet you at the wagons?"

Beany shifted his hundred and ninety pounds uneasily in the chair. "Just seemed like we ought to get acquainted again over some coffee. It's been nigh into three years since Abe or me has seen you, Jeff."

Jeff nodded. He felt that he was still well enough acquainted with Beany to know that he was hiding something.

"When can I see this big three-wagon train?" he asked.

"Any time," Beany said quickly. "I've already hired the drivers. That kid, Norrie Fergison, that I sent out to find you, is one. A fellow named Hod Terpko is the other one. I—I may drive the other wagon myself."

Jeff noticed the hesitation in Beany but he was as hard to pin down as a wet snake. Grilli was still on Jeff's mind, anyway.

"Have you heard of Ross Grilli out there in Colorado?"

Beany shook his head. "Denver ain't too far from the ranch but we don't get up there often so we don't hear much news. We have a new man named Gossy working on the AR now. He don't talk much, though, so he's no source of news."

Jeff frowned again. Beany was talking too much and saying too little. That wasn't like him. He'd known Beany since he was twelve when he'd gone to live with Abe and Miranda back in Missouri. It seemed to Jeff that Beany must have been with Abe since time began, although Beany couldn't be much over forty now. His almost bald head with its fringe of brown hair and that extra weight on his five foot seven inch frame added to his look of age.

A big man came across the room and stopped at the table. Jeff looked up and was startled at the piercing gleam in the gray eyes he met. The man was about the same height as Jeff, six feet, but he was twenty or thirty pounds heavier. Jeff guessed him to be a little younger than he was.

"This is Hod Terpko," Beany said. "My other driver. This is the wagon boss, Jeff Ryan," he said to Terpko.

Terpko ran his eyes over Jeff and Jeff felt a wave of animosity. Was he getting it from Terpko? He didn't usually dislike a man on sight.

"You're the wagon boss?" Terpko said. "Are you sure you know which end of a wagon to hitch the team to?"

"I was just wondering if you knew which end of a

horse to feed," Jeff shot back. He looked Terpko over as steadily as the big man was eyeing him.

Terpko didn't look like a driver to Jeff. But he'd seen some strange men handling the reins on wagons headed west. Terpko would not be the strangest. He might be better suited to the job than a grocer or banker taking his wagon west to start up a new business. A hired driver, though, ought to be familiar with all the chores associated with his job. Jeff doubted if Terpko was.

"When do we start for Colorado?" Terpko asked.

"Beany hasn't told me yet," Jeff said.

"Thought you was the wagon boss."

"I will be when we hit the road," Jeff said. "I hope you don't forget that."

"I ain't liable to," Terpko said and moved on.

"You two hit it off like a couple of range bulls that got pushed into the same pasture," Beany said after Terpko was gone.

"He rubs me wrong," Jeff said.

"He isn't too sociable," Beany admitted. "But I needed a driver and he wanted a job. Said he could handle a team well."

"How about taking a look at the wagons?" Jeff asked.

Beany nodded. "Let's go. I just wanted you to understand your uncle's proposition. A partnership in the AR if you take this train through. But if you back out, you get nothing."

"Agreed," Jeff said. "Now let's take a look."

Outside the restaurant, Jeff got the horse he had

bought with the money he'd had in his pocket after Grilli made off with his horse and what money Jeff had had stored away. Beany went to his gray mule he called Angel. He'd had that mule the last time Jeff had seen him when Jeff had stopped at the AR between trail jobs. He'd fallen in love with Abe's ranch on that visit.

"Come on, Samson," Beany called to his mongrel dog that had gone over to lie in the shade of a scrub tree while waiting for his master.

Jeff thought that Beany made a ridiculous sight here on the streets of Kansas City, riding a mule. slumped in his saddle, a slouch hat pulled down over his bald head with just a fringe of brown hair showing underneath, and a mongrel dog trailing behind the mule.

It wasn't a long ride to the three canvas-topped wagons. Jeff was more puzzled than ever as to why Beany had ridden to town to meet him at the restaurant. These wagons were closer to Jeff's camp than the restaurant.

Jeff expected to see a few men around the camp but he saw only one, Norrie. The other driver, Terpko, must still be in town. But then he saw something that made him jerk back on the reins of his horse.

"What are all those women doing there?" he demanded.

"Going to Colorado," Beany said as matter-of-factly as possible.

"Not in those wagons," Jeff said, feeling as if a mule had kicked him.

"They ain't going to walk," Beany said.

"There's enough women there for two dozen wagons," Jeff muttered.

"Only six," Beany corrected.

"Why are they going?"

"Same reason women go anywhere—men," Beany said. "They're the cargo."

"A petticoat wagon train!" Jeff exclaimed. "Not with me as boss."

"You said you'd do it," Beany half shouted. "Abe's banking on you."

"You didn't say anything about a load of women."

"You didn't ask."

"So that's why you had me meet you in town," Jeff exploded. "You knew I wouldn't ride herd on a trail full of women."

Beany rubbed his chin. "Sort of figured it that way. But Abe's going to skin me if I don't bring you."

"Then leave those women here."

"He'll draw and quarter me if I don't bring them. He sent for them."

"Abe?" Jeff roared. "Is he out of his mind?"

"They ain't for him," Beany said indignantly. "They're for his cowboys. It seems every time we hire some young bucks, they go off to Denver to find wine, women and song and don't come back for a week or longer. He figures if they're all married, they'll stay put on the AR."

Jeff shook his head. "What do the boys think about that?"

"They're for it whole hog."

Jeff stared at Beany. "And Abe let you pick them out?"

13

Beany bristled. "I may be a little past my prime but I ain't blind. You get close enough, you'll see. They're pretty. And I ain't dumb, either. I picked some good ones."

Jeff sighed. "I hate to let Uncle Abe down. But I want no part of train full of women. That would be worse than fighting the Big War again."

"You promised," Beany reminded. "Abe will be plenty mad when I tell him you broke your promise."

"I didn't promise to boss no women."

"Ain't no man alive can really boss a woman," Beany said. "But you can manage to keep them from killing each other till we get there. I'll help you see to it they don't do nothing to wreck the train."

"I'd have less trouble hauling a wagon lead of pussy cats," Jeff grunted.

"Not unless you threw in some tom cats," Beany said.

"Do you figure you and Terpko and Norrie and me are pussy cats, too?"

Beany shook his head. "You've got a point. They *are* the marrying kind, or they wouldn't have agreed to come. But no woman has ever caught either one of us. I reckon we can get them to Colorado without being hooked. Anyway, you've got to do it; it's my hide if you don't. You want that partnership; you want to help Abe; you're down and out."

Beany was voicing the very arguments that Jeff was running through his mind. He did want that partnership with Abe. He loved that ranch. His wagon boss days were over and he knew it.

He'd had some strange people in some of the trains he'd guided across the plains. Surely he could get this bunch of women to Colorado some way. It wouldn't take long. It wasn't like going to Oregon. He'd worked lots harder for a lot less than a partnership in a ranch like the AR. He knew Abe well enough to know that if he said he wouldn't give him a share in the ranch if he didn't bring the wagons through, he'd stick by that decision.

"All right," he said finally. "My good sense tells me to keep hands off but I'll do it for Uncle Abe."

"And yourself," Beany added.

"I'm going back and get my stuff from my camp."

"Don't you want to look over the cargo?"

"I'll see plenty of that before we get to Colorado."

Jeff reined his horse around and headed him across the prairie toward the camp he had left this morning. He hadn't mentioned just now his most important reason for going. Somewhere in Colorado was Ross Grilli. As soon as he was settled on the AR, he'd get some time off and go to Denver and look for Grilli. He didn't doubt that Grilli was in Denver right now spending the money he'd taken from Jeff, if he had any of it left.

He came to the draw where he'd seen Norrie first this morning. Just over the ridge was his camp. But the camp was suddenly driven from his mind as three masked riders charged at him from the draw.

He wheeled his horse and clawed for his gun but they already had guns on him and he took his hand away empty. Then they were on him. One man grabbed him by the shoulders and literally threw him from the saddle. He landed on his back and his horse shied away.

Two of the men hit the ground before Jeff could get up. The other one watched from his seat in the saddle. Jeff's first thought was that they intended to rob him because they were masked. That would be a joke on them. He didn't have anything. But then they charged at him and one man aimed a kick at his ribs.

He rolled away but before he could get up, they were on him and began pounding him with sledge-hammer blows. He realized with a touch of panic that they would kill him if they kept this up.

II

Pain shot through his side as a fist connected solidly with his ribs. Another blow snapped his head around. A fog clouded his thinking but through it came the sharp realization that he had to get out from under the two men or they would kill him.

He struck out blindly with all the force he could muster and rocked one of the men with a blow to the side of the head. The man evidently hadn't expected any retaliation for the punishment he was dealing out and he lost his balance and lunged backward to catch himself.

Jeff clawed for his gun but the other man lashed out with a boot and caught Jeff on the wrist. The gun spurted out of his hand and over the bank toward the creek.

Jeff expected to see one of them pull a gun now. He had pushed the battle to those limits himself. But the two men were lunging at him again barehanded. Maybe they were just too close to town and other camps to risk using a gun. With their victim unarmed now, they really didn't need guns.

Jeff fought furiously but he was strictly on the defensive and he was outnumbered. He knew he was going to lose this battle. That didn't prevent him from inflicting as much punishment as he possibly could.

Suddenly the man still on his horse called sharply. "Don't kill him. We just want him to understand that he ain't going to Colorado. If he tries it, he'll get worse than he got today."

Jeff's head was ringing from the blows he'd taken but he heard and understood what the man was saying. Why were they trying to stop him from going to Colorado? His brain was too fuzzy to find an answer.

The men wheeled to their horses and Jeff, his mind on his gun, rolled over the bank into the sand at the edge of the water. Looking around frantically, he spotted his gun right in the edge of the water, barrel probbed into the mud and sand.

Jerking the gun free, he scrambled to his feet to peer over the bank at the three men. They were already riding up the draw. Jeff had enough mind left to know that he didn't dare fire his gun until he cleaned the mud out of the barrel.

Gingerly, he climbed back up the bank to his horse. He hurt all over. Pulling himself onto his horse, he rode toward his camp, only a short distance away. There, he gathered up his few belongings, then paused long enough to clean his gun before mounting again and riding back toward the wagons.

The warning not to go to Colorado lingered in his mind but staying here rather than going to Abe's ranch with Beany and his wagons just didn't rate any consideration with him. The only logical explanation for the warning was that Ross Grilli had sent the men to make sure he didn't follow him to Colorado.

But if Grilli hadn't sent them, then they must have some reason for not wanting him to guide those wagons west. But how could they know that he was going to guide Beany's wagons? He had just taken the job an hour ago. Besides, why would anybody want to stop those wagons from going to Colorado?

Seeing Beany at the rear of the nearest wagon, Jeff headed straight for him. Beany studied his face as he dismounted.

"Looks like somebody mistook your face for a slab of beef and was getting it ready for the skillet," he said.

Jeff explained the fight. "Any idea who might have jumped me?"

Beany shook his head, frowning. "Sure don't. No reason why anybody should object to you taking these girls west. They all want to go and they're old enough to decide for themselves."

"Must be because of the girls, though," Jeff said.

"Let's look them over and you decide," Beany suggested. "You'll need to get acquainted with them, anyway."

"I figure I can live without it," Jeff muttered. But he

followed Beany toward the wagons. He noticed that Terpko had gotten back from town. He looked as surly as ever.

The girls were clustered near the center wagon and standing in front of them was a big woman, about forty years old. Jeff stared at her in surprise. She was actually a little taller than Beany and a few pounds heavier. She wore a long dress that made Jeff think of an animated tent. But it was her scowl and piercing eyes that really caught his attention.

"I thought you said you were taking girls out there," Jeff said softly. "That one is no girl."

"That's Bessie Scarpitta," Beany said. "She is the chaperon for the girls."

Jeff nodded. "That makes sense. She could stand off an army."

"That ain't no joke," Beany muttered. "She also hired on to drive the girls' wagon. The front wagon will have our gear in it and the cooking stuff. This one in the back holds the girls' trunks. They brought everything they owned 'cause they don't figure on coming back. Norrie will drive this one; Terpko the one up front."

Jeff halted. "We're close enough," he said. "You tell me about the girls. Any problems I should know about?"

Beany frowned. "I want you to meet them; not just stare at them. If there are any problems, I figure Bessie will be it. Come on."

Jeff followed Beany up to Bessie and acknowledged the introduction. Bessie looked Jeff over like a cattle buyer judging a beef.

"I suppose you're going to try bossing us around," Bessie challenged.

"If I'm going to be wagon boss, I'll be the boss," Jeff said. "If you stay where you belong and don't cause trouble, I won't have any orders to give."

"Now mister, let me tell you something," Bessie said. "I'll do my job. You do yours. But if you come messing around my territory, I'll give some orders and you'll understand them, too."

Jeff eyed the woman. She was one who enjoyed a good fight, he guessed. Before they got to Colorado, she'd probably get it from somebody.

"If you mean your girls, don't worry," Jeff said.

He and Beany moved on toward the wagon. "You made that sound bad, Jeff," Beany complained. "These aren't her girls. She's just chaperon."

They came to the girls and Beany's face beamed. He was proud of them; it showed in his face and voice.

"This is Cheery Yandall, the youngest one," he said. "Her pa is a preacher. She came to Kansas City to get a job but jobs aren't very plentiful. She liked the idea of going to the Rockies to marry a cowboy."

Jeff looked at the auburn haired girl with the hazel eyes. She was pretty. Likely this was the alternative she had to a life she didn't want. Maybe Beany had done her a favor. He guessed she wasn't over eighteen or nineteen.

"Please to meet you, Mr. Ryan," she said softly.

"Same here," he said. He doubted if he'd have any trouble with Cheery.

20

"This is Lily Quirk," Beany said, moving over in front of the tallest girl Jeff had seen in a long time. She was within an inch of his height. She wasn't heavy for her size but he'd guess she was plenty strong for a woman.

"Happy to see a man as tall as me," Lily said in a voice that could have been mistaken for a man's.

"She was a teacher in Kansas City," Beany said. "A school of one looked better to her than a room full of kids."

"Could wind up with both," Lily added with a shrug.

"This is Posey McRae," Beany said, moving on. "She's looking forward to snagging herself a cowboy."

Jeff looked at the small red-headed, blue-eyed girl, rather plump compared to the others. He guessed her to be well past twenty, maybe twenty-three or -four. If he was any judge of girls, this one had been around. She had none of the innocent look of Cheery.

Beany's face softened as he moved down the line. "Here is Tonalia Kemp. We all call her Toni. Had a stepfather at home who tried to work her to death. She ran off but couldn't find any work she wanted in Kansas City."

"You think ranch work will be easier?" Jeff asked. Tonalia was the smallest girl in the group, barely five feet tall and he guessed she wouldn't tip the scales much more than a hundred pounds. She had bright blonde hair with sky blue eyes. Some lucky cowboy was going to get a mighty pretty wife.

"It will be honest work, at least," Tonalia said.

"The last one here is Star Unser," Beany said, indi-

21

cating a medium tall girl with black hair and eyes. "She lost her husband in the war and has been working as a housekeeper and cook since then."

"I might as well be doing that work in my own home," Star said. She looked sharply at Jeff. "Since it's your uncle's ranch we're going to, maybe you can tell us something about the men there. Is there one who would accept a little boy who wasn't his own?"

"I don't know Uncle Abe's men that well," Jeff said. "But if you've got a son, you'd better make sure the man you pick will take the boy before you marry him."

"There's more than just the boy," Beany said hesitantly. "She has three goats along."

Jeff wheeled on Beany. "She has the boy and the goats with her?"

"Not the boy," Beany said hastily. "She left him with some relatives. But she's got the goats."

"A doctor put me on goat's milk a couple of years ago," Star said simply. "I don't have to have it now but I like it. So I brought my goats along."

Jeff frowned. "Goats are one thing that I never liked on a train. Where are they?"

"The nanny goats are tied on the other side of the wagon. The billy goat won't leave while they're tied up."

Jeff's scowl deepened. "A billy goat? I sure don't like that."

"Billy goats don't bite," Beany said uneasily.

"It's not his teeth that worries me," Jeff said.

Beany headed back toward the rear wagon and Jeff followed. His introduction to the girls hadn't eased his foreboding. Beany was right about one thing. The girls were pretty. Two of them, Cheery and Tonalia, were more than just pretty; they were beautiful. Jeff had learned long ago that a pretty girl on a wagon train created problems, especially among the men. A wagon load of unattached pretty girls suggested more trouble than Jeff cared to contemplate.

"Now that you've had your look," Bessie said as they passed her, "keep your distance."

Jeff stopped and glared at the big woman. "I'll be giving the orders in this train," he snapped. "You keep the girls in line and I guarantee you I won't bother them."

"A woman hater, huh?" Bessie snorted. "That suits me fine." She turned on Beany. "Why did you bring that Posey along?"

"She wants to marry a cowboy," Beany said. "Why else?"

"That's what I asked you," Bessie said, frowning. "You know what she is, don't you?"

"She's a girl heading west to get married," Beany said stubbornly.

Bessie snorted. "When they passed out the brains, you must have been hiding under a thimble."

"She says she's a cook," Beany said.

"All she'll cook up on this trip is a mess of trouble."

Jeff wouldn't have argued with Bessie's evaluation but he saw that Beany was about ready to explode so he moved on, hoping Beany would follow. He did.

"I should have fired her before I hired her," Beany muttered. "She gives more orders than an army general. Expects them to be followed, too."

"Why *did* you hire her?" Jeff said.

"She asked for the job," Beany said defensively. "I needed a driver and a chaperon for the girls. She's both. She's also the best cook in Kansas City. She was cooking at a boarding house where I stayed so I know."

"Why did she leave that job?"

" 'Cause Cheery is her niece. Cheery doesn't know it. Bessie is the black sheep sister of Cheery's pa, the preacher. She wants to go along to make sure nothing happens to Cheery. I liked the idea."

"She may be right about Posey causing trouble," Jeff said.

"There was a special reason for bringing Posey," Beany said, "a reason I ain't going to tell even you."

Jeff checked the loads, rearranging some. The wagons looked good enough to make the trip to Colorado without trouble. He saw Hod Terpko go over the center wagon once but he ran into Bessie and he retreated without an argument. Bessie might prove to be a blessing in disguise. She was the one thing that could keep trouble down as they headed west.

Bessie took charge as head cook for the camp with the girls helping. Star was the best help once she had milked her goats. Posey did the least, even though she was listed as a cook.

After supper, Bessie left the girls to wash the pots and pans and came over to Jeff. "You ain't starting out tomorrow, are you?"

"Why not? We want to get there as soon as possible."

"Tomorrow's Friday," Bessie said, shaking her head.

"It's just asking for trouble to start anything on Friday that you can't finish before sundown."

Jeff frowned. "Are you superstitious?"

"Just careful," Bessie said. "Better think about laying over another day."

Bessie and the girls set up a tent on the far side of their wagon. Jeff asked Beany about that.

"For their baths," Beany said disgustedly. "Bessie says they want baths and we'd better be sure to camp close to a creek so they can have them."

Jeff discovered another arrangement when morning came. In exchange for cooking, Bessie expected the men to hitch up and unhitch her teams and take care of the horses. It was a fair exchange, he decided, because Bessie and the girls were good cooks.

In spite of Bessie's misgivings, Jeff got the three wagons on the road shortly after sun-up. They hadn't gone a mile until Jeff saw that Norrie was a better driver than Terpko. Hod Terpko didn't appear to know anything about handling a team. Jeff caught him glaring at him a couple of times when he happened to look that way quickly.

"What's eating Terpko?" Jeff asked Beany. "Acts like he hates me."

"I don't know what ails him. He ain't much of a driver like he said he was, that's sure. Ought to fire him but I might have trouble finding anybody to take his place."

"Reckon I can handle him," Jeff said. "But I'd like to know why he asked for this job."

The day went much better than Jeff had expected for

the first day out. He found a good campsite near a creek with a high bank and called a halt early, giving the travelers a short day to settle into the routine of traveling.

He helped unhitch Bessie's team and he heard Bessie giving the girls strict orders to stay close to the wagon. If they objected to the orders, they didn't voice their opinions.

It was shortly after supper and darkness had settled down when Jeff heard a cry from the direction of the creek. He shot a glance at the center wagon. He could see only one girl and Bessie. Were the other four in the wagon? Or was one down by the creek?

The cry came again, sounding like a woman half yelling, half screaming. Jeff headed that way, pulling his gun out of the holster as he ran. He didn't know which girl was in trouble; it didn't make any difference.

He had momentarily forgotten the high cliff on which they were camped. He had heard some grumbling because water had to be carried from a hundred yards upstream where they could get down to the creek. Now suddenly he caught his toe on a limb in his path. He felt himself falling and he couldn't catch himself.

It was then that he remembered the cliff. He was going over it and it was a long drop. He could break some bones, maybe his neck.

III

He hit an outcropping of rock, bruising his hip. It flashed through his mind that he had thought the cliff was perpendicular and there would be nothing for him to touch until he hit the rubble at the base of the bluff close to the creek.

His grasping fingers caught a bush rooted on the rock ledge. He was still near the top of the cliff and had not gained much momentum. Still the strain on the roots of the bush was terrific, but it held. For a moment Jeff hung there, wondering what second the bush would let go and spill him onto the rubble below.

He heard rocks still dribbling onto the rubble while he dangled there in the dark. He didn't hear the cry again that had brought him dashing out this way but he did hear footsteps pounding across the prairie above him. Someone from the wagons had heard the noise he'd made falling over the cliff and dislodging the rocks or else they, too, were coming in response to the cry that had brought Jeff out here.

He yelled, as much to keep anyone else from falling over the cliff as to bring help. The yell directed the approaching steps to the edge of the cliff above him.

"You down there, Jeff?" Beany yelled.

"Right here," Jeff said, only a few feet below Beany. "Hanging onto a bush that may go any second."

"I'll get a rope," Beany said and Jeff heard him running back toward the wagons.

When he returned, there were others with him. The bush was still holding. Jeff felt the rope hit him as Beany lowered it. With his free hand, he grasped it and made sure he had a good grip before he yelled up to Beany that he had it.

When Beany called that they had the rope anchored, Jeff let go of the bush and swung free on the rope. Getting his feet braced against the cliff, he helped himself up by walking against the cliff while those above kept the rope tight.

As Jeff reached the top and threw himself on the ground away from the brink of the cliff, he saw a lantern bobbing toward him. Bessie was swinging it manfully as she came from the wagons.

"Couldn't wait for a light, could you?" Bessie demanded of Beany when she arrived.

"If you'd been hanging down there, I might have waited for sun-up," Beany muttered.

Bessie stepped to the edge and held the lantern over. The weak beam from the lantern didn't reach the bottom but everyone knew what was down there. Beany shook his head.

"You wouldn't be among the living, Jeff, if you hadn't caught that bush," he said solemnly. "Didn't you know that cliff was there?"

"I forgot," Jeff admitted. "But I wouldn't have fallen over the edge if I hadn't tripped on something."

Bessie swung the lantern around. The light revealed a branch of a tree off to one side where Jeff's boot had kicked it when he tripped over it.

"How did that get up here where there ain't no

trees?" Beany asked.

"Looks like somebody carried it up here sometime," Terpko said. "Maybe some Indian brought it up for his campfire."

"Sure didn't burn it," Beany said. "Where were you when we heard that scream?"

"Checking the horses," Terpko said quickly. "I was coming this way when I heard the rocks falling."

Jeff looked at the girls clustered around and behind Bessie. A quick count showed all of them there. Norrie was there, too, so everyone was accounted for. He looked at Beany and saw the suspicion on his face in the flickering light.

As they turned toward the wagon, Tonalia dropped back beside Jeff. "I was out here when I came for water," she said. "I liked the view from the top of this bluff. I'm sure there wasn't any tree limb here then because I was looking for something to burn."

Jeff nodded. This confirmed his suspicions. Someone had deliberately set up this trap. Whoever did it knew that a cry from the creek would bring people on the run. And they could almost be sure that Jeff would be the first one to respond. They couldn't be sure that he would stumble over the tree limb and go over the bluff but the limb was positioned so that if he did hit it, he would certainly go over.

"You weren't down along the creek just now?"

Toni shook her head. "I was in the wagon trying to read by this lantern. Bessie came for the lantern and I followed her here."

"Were all the rest of the girls at the wagon?"

Toni thought a moment then nodded. "Lily was just finishing her bath. The rest of us were either in the wagon or right next to it." She stared at Jeff. "You don't think one of us screamed?"

"It sounded like a woman's scream and you girls and Bessie have a corner on that product."

"It did sound like a woman screaming," Toni said after a minute. "But it wasn't any of us."

"I'll figure it out," Jeff said. "Glad you told me about that limb."

Toni joined the other girls and Jeff sought out Beany. While the camp settled down again, Jeff and Beany talked a short distance from the rear wagon.

"That was set up," Jeff said. "Looks like it was aimed at me."

Beany nodded. "I figured that. What I can't figure is why anybody would be trying to kill or cripple you."

"It's the second try. Everyone in camp can give an account of himself—unless it was Norrie."

"He was with me when we heard that squall," Beany said. "Terpko was with the horses—or says he was—and the girls and Bessie were all at their wagon."

"A man could have made that scream, I guess," Jeff said. "None of us was paying that much attention."

"Could have been somebody from Kansas City," Beany said. "We're only a day away. That's not too far to come for someone who wanted to kill or cripple a man."

"I can't think of anyone who would like to see me dead except Ross Grilli. He knows I'm likely to trail him to Colorado."

30

"Nobody out there knows I was coming after you except Abe's hands. And nobody, not even the AR cowboys, knows Abe is planning to make you his partner. This Grilli you keep talking about must be the kind of friend a man can do without."

"We were partners on our last trip to Oregon," Jeff explained. "I was wagon boss; he was the scout and guide. In western Nebraska, I saw a side of him I didn't like. We'd been attacked by Indians and we captured a wounded buck. Ross had been scratched by an arrow and he was mad. He took it out on that Indian, beating him then killing him before we could interfere. He has a vicious temper."

"Nice partner you had! Why did he turn on you?"

"I saw him steal some money from a wagon. Those people didn't have much and I made him give it back. He was madder than a dog in a briar patch. We had a fight and I licked him. He swore he'd get even with me. I expected him to try because he nurses a grudge like he was its mother."

"Is that when he stole your horse and money?"

"Shortly after we got back to Kansas City," Jeff said. "And I doubt if that satisfied him. If he knew I was on my way to Colorado, he'd do anything to keep me from getting there."

"No way he could know that," Beany said.

"Well, somebody is trying to kill or cripple me, that's sure."

"If I was you, I wouldn't trust no one," Beany warned.

Morning brought confusion as they broke camp. This would settle down into a routine about the activity. It wasn't helped any by Beany's dog, Samson, and Star's billy goat. She called her goat Hercules, Jeff had learned. And the two nanny goats were Athena and Diana. Jeff's skimpy knowledge of mythology placed those names of Greek or Roman goddesses. Hercules was a Greek god. The goats looked like anything but gods to Jeff. And they were even less appealing to Beany, especially when Hercules took a special dislike to Samson. The feeling appeared to be mutual.

"Samson loves that goat about like an Indian loves smallpox," Beany said. "I'd like to barbecue that horned son of Satan but nobody could eat him."

Most goats would keep out of the way of a dog but Hercules gave ground to absolutely nothing. He defiantly stamped the ground and shook his head at Samson. Samson was not a fighting dog but he was no coward, either, and he didn't propose to let Hercules rule the camp.

"Keep your ding-busted goat away from my dog," Beany yelled at Star.

"Keep your dog away from my goat," Star retorted spiritedly.

"Why don't you tie up the billy goat and let the nannies run free?" Jeff suggested.

"They might run off," Star said. "But Hercules won't leave while Diana and Athena are with the wagons. Besides, Hercules is my bodyguard."

"I can think of a lot better names for him," Beany muttered.

Jeff foresaw trouble with two stubborn animals like Hercules and Samson running loose in camp, both determined to be kingpin. But the first dose of trouble came sooner than he anticipated.

The wagons were loaded and the teams hitched up when Hercules came around the wagon where the nanny goats were tied and confronted Samson waiting beside Angel and Beany. Samson growled his displeasure and Hercules shook his head, his whiskers flying, his menacing horns slashing the air.

Samson didn't give ground when the goat moved closer. Instead, he dived at the goat's heels. The goat wheeled and in a moment there was a general melee. Beany had been standing beside Angel checking the cinch on the saddle. He began yelling at Samson to run.

Samson was in no mood to run. Neither was Hercules. If Beany had just mounted Angel and ridden out, Samson might have broken free and followed. But Beany tried to rescue his dog from those sharp horns, diving into the melee to get Samson free. In the process, he got butted very unceremoniously by the goat.

Jeff couldn't believe what he was seeing. It was almost impossible to distinguish any one of the combatants. There were bleats, barks and curses flowing out of the melee like water bubbling out of a spring.

It finally broke up when Hercules got a horn hooked in Beany's shirt. Samson, free at last from the menace of those horns, took a good nip at Hercules' heels. Hercules threw up his head and bleated in pain and charged away, taking Beany as far as the shirt would hold out. When it ripped, Beany hit the ground with a thud punctuated with some language not meant for the mixed company witnessing the scramble. But the fight was over.

"Watch your tongue!" Bessie screamed at Beany.

Beany got up and glared at Bessie. "You watch what—that—smelly son of Beelzebub!" he yelled back. "You can just patch this shirt tonight."

"I'll do that," Star said quickly.

"Why did you get into the scrap, Beany?" Jeff asked.

Bessie answered before Beany could say a word. "That's easy to figure. Two billy goats and a dog made an evener match."

"*Two* billy goats!" Beany exploded. "Woman, I'll tie you out here and let that goat butt you all the way to Colorado."

"Like the—the dickens you will!" Bessie roared.

Jeff had the feeling she'd have used much stronger language herself but remembered her assumed position of chaperon just in time.

The train moved out and Samson and Hercules maintained a respectable distance from each other. Jeff had the feeling they wouldn't tangle again unless circumstances pushed them together where one would have to show cowardice and avoid a fight. Neither animal was going to do that. They were like some people, Jeff thought.

They stopped at noon for dinner and to let the horses rest and graze. There were pebbles on the knoll where they had halted the wagon. Jeff saw Terpko pick up some of the small rocks and toss them one at a time at Hercules. The goat flinched when one hit him and wheeled, looking for his tormentor. But Terpko would never be looking his way and gave no indication he was to blame. The goat was fooled but he was also angry and looking for a target on which to vent his wrath.

Jeff saw the agitated goat stamping around, bleating his fury. He started toward Terpko but Terpko turned and walked away to get his team. Jeff let him go. He had little love for the goat but an irritated goat could mean more trouble for everyone.

Jeff rode ahead late in the afternoon and found a good place to camp. The wagons were lined up for the night and Bessie was busy with supper when Jeff noticed that Hercules was stalking toward something or somebody near the creek. Jeff wondered if the goat was still angry from the teasing he had endured at the noon stop.

Suddenly the goat charged. Jeff heard a scream then a splash. He headed that way on the run. One of the girls was in the creek, that was sure.

Coming around some bushes, he saw Hercules at the edge of the water, shaking his head angrily, looking out at Tonalia splashing furiously in the water, ten feet from the shoreline. The water was swift and Toni was wearing a long dress that was rapidly catching the water like a sail catches the wind.

Jeff charged straight at the goat, which was directly between him and Toni. Hercules heard Jeff coming and wheeled to defend himself. But he seemed to sense the fury in Jeff and hastily decided that an honorable retreat was in order. With an angry bleat, he left the creek and headed back toward camp on a circuitous route.

The river was winning its battle with Toni and she was starting to move with the current in spite of her furious struggles. Jeff didn't take time even to kick off his boots. He plunged into the water and forced his way out to a spot where he could grab onto that flowing skirt which hadn't all been soaked enough to sink beneath the water.

Toni was the smallest of the five girls and Jeff had no trouble pulling her to him and carrying her back to the river bank. She was frightened but not hysterical as he thought all women were supposed to be in such circumstances. Everyone from the wagons was on the bank when he got Toni there.

"You're going to have to do something with that goat," he said sharply to Star.

"The wind must have been blowing her skirt," Star said. "Hercules butts anything that waves at him."

"How about the business end of a six-gun?" Beany growled.

Star ignored Beany as the girls took Toni toward their wagon. Jeff headed for the rear wagon where he had some changes of clothes. He stifled an urge to kick the goat when he passed him near the wagons.

Before he finished changing clothes, he heard a swelling, low-voiced excitement outside. He hurriedly pulled on his dry pants and boots and stepped outside. A rather small man, looking smaller than he was because of the big bay horse he was riding, had stopped near the lead wagon. With his long-tailed black coat and bow tie, he looked as out of place as a toad at a banquet.

Beany saw Jeff and retreated to him. "Says his name is Ivie," he said in a low voice. "Came from the west. Trying to tell us what a rough time he has had. Don't look in such bad shape to me."

Jeff nodded and strode forward. The man had dismounted now and Jeff saw that he was about the size of Norrie. He stepped forward, obviously recognizing Jeff as the leader here.

"Name is Orrin Ivie," the man said. "I'm heading back to Kansas City. Saw your camp and thought I'd stop by. Sort of riding the chuck line, you might say."

"You're welcome to supper," Jeff said. "What are you doing out here?"

"I started west with a train," Ivie said easily. "Decided I'd be more comfortable back at my table in the Green Lantern in Kansas City. So I got my horse and turned back."

Jeff looked over the fancy dressed man. "I'd say you made a wise decision."

He turned back to Bessie but she had already returned to the cooking fire, muttering to herself. Jeff caught a glimpse of Posey disappearing around the center wagon. He was sure he had seen fear in her face. He wheeled back to look at Ivie but if Ivie had noticed Posey, he gave no sign of it. He was already telling a gory tale of what he had seen to the west in an Indian battle.

Jeff scowled. They were entirely too far east to be troubled by Indians. Ivie hadn't ridden that far, either.

Something about the man didn't add up. But his stories were frightening the girls half out of their wits. Jeff frowned. Orrin Ivie's stories could cause trouble.

IV

During the supper, Ivie kept up a steady chatter, telling wild stories of happenings on the trail. Jeff watched the reaction of the girls. None of them had ever been west of the Missouri River before and they were taking it all in as if it were the unvarnished truth. Seeing the fear growing in the faces of the listeners, Jeff called a halt.

"You're welcome to the supper and to spend the night here, Mr. Ivie," he said. "But lay off the wild stories. You've got these girls believing what you say."

"Why not?" Ivie said innocently. "It's the truth."

Jeff stood up, towering over Ivie, who was still sitting on the ground. "I've been traveling these plains for over ten years, Mister. I know what's out there. You're lying like a tinhorn."

Ivie uncoiled and sprang up like a jack-in-the-box. "Nobody calls me a tinhorn," he snapped.

"Then don't act like one," Jeff said, glaring at him. "You are a gambler, aren't you?"

"Not a tinhorn gambler," Ivie shouted.

"Maybe not," Jeff said. "But you're a liar when you say the Indians are on the warpath and have burned Fort Hays. And you say you were captured but you talked your way out of trouble while they tortured two others to death. If you'd talked half as much in their camp as you have here, they'd have burned you at the stake just to shut you up."

Ivie wilted and turned toward his horse. "Guess I know when I'm not welcome," he said.

Jeff looked around at the girls. Posey hadn't shown up even for supper. Lily said she wasn't feeling well. Jeff guessed she was afraid of Ivie. He wanted to know why. He followed Ivie to his horse.

"Do you know any of those girls back there?" he asked.

Ivie looked at him innocently. "How would I know any of them?"

"I didn't ask how. I asked if. You're from Kansas City; so are they. You might have seen them there."

Ivie shrugged. "I see a lot of people. I could have seen one of them but I doubt it."

Jeff had the feeling he was lying like he had been about the Indians. He turned back to the wagons. When he didn't hear Ivie's horse leaving camp, he turned to look and saw Hod Terpko talking to Ivie. That stirred more uneasy feelings in Jeff. He must be getting jumpy. Bossing a wagon train of women was more nerve-racking than a big train of emigrants.

Posey came out of the wagon shortly after Ivie had ridden away. Jeff found the opportunity to ask her about Ivie.

"I don't know anything about him," she said shortly. "I saw him once. He is a gambler at the Green Lantern. He has no business out here."

Jeff nodded. "Sort of figured that myself. But that

doesn't explain why he is here."

Posey knew Ivie better than she would admit, Jeff would bet. Why she was so afraid of him was something he'd better find out. If Ivie had come into camp to find Posey, he likely knew now that she was here. What would he do about it? A lot might depend on why he was looking for her.

Jeff found Bessie cleaning up some pans near the fire. As self-appointed chaperon of the girls, she should know something about them.

"Ever seen Orrin Ivie before?" he asked her.

She shook her head. "Posey has, though."

"I figured that. What do you know about her?"

"That she ain't got no business on this trip. She ain't the marrying kind."

"Do you know what connection Posey has with Ivie?"

"Don't know that there is one. But I'll keep an eye on her and find out why she's scared of him if I can. What about these Indian raids that gambler was talking about?"

"We're too far east to be worrying about Indians. There isn't much trouble with Indians anywhere now."

"I hope not," Bessie said dubiously. "The girls are pretty worked up about it—especially Lily."

"Tell them not to worry," Jeff said and moved on toward his bedroll.

Beany had the first watch and Jeff would take the second one. He wasn't sure that Ivie might not try to sneak back into camp if he was after Posey. But the night passed without any alarm and the wagon train moved on the next morning.

There was a tension in the train today that hadn't been there yesterday. Jeff attributed that to those wild stories of Indian raids that Ivie had told. His assurances that there were no Indians this far east hadn't been able to quiet the fears of the girls. They passed an occasional farm and they saw two little towns during the day. But still the fears persisted.

Jeff selected a nice meadow close to a stream for the evening camp. He made sure they were some distance from any trees that could be used by an enemy to sneak in close. His precaution was aimed at any maneuver that Orrin Ivie might initiate against the train. Another day or two out on the trail and he could probably forget about Ivie following them farther. He was a city man.

The security of the campsite was noted carefully by Bessie and the girls and they interpreted it as a precaution against an Indian raid. Bessie, in particular, prepared for the worst. She got out the rifles she had stored in the girls' wagon and made quite a show of checking each one and loading it. Then she handed a loaded rifle to each girl with instructions on how to use it.

"What's all the fuss?" Jeff asked, hoping to quiet the fears showing in the girls.

"You heard what that gambler said," Bessie said. "Well, back there this morning when we passed that farm house, a black cat ran across the road in front of us. And if that wasn't enough, did you see that ladder propped up against the west wall of that farm house we

41

passed not a mile back there?"

Jeff shrugged. "What about it?"

Bessie snorted. "If you don't know that means bad luck, then there's no use telling you anything. But me and the girls are going to be prepared for that bad luck."

Jeff was uneasy but not for the same superstitious reasons that governed Bessie's preparations. If Ivie intended to try to get to Posey, he'd do it soon. Each day they were getting farther from Kansas City and Jeff didn't think Ivie would range too far from his familiar gambling tables.

If he was expecting an Indian attack, he'd look for it at dawn. He wasn't sure what to expect from Ivie, if anything at all. When the night passed without incident, he began to relax. But he discovered that was premature.

A wild whoop shattered the dawn and Jeff grabbed his rifle as he threw back his blanket. Terpko was on guard now. Norrie and Beany joined Jeff in running out beyond the wagons in the direction the yell had come from.

"Indians!" Terpko shouted, retreating to the wagons.

"Funny sounding Indians," Beany said. "But here they come!"

As the riders came closer, firing their rifles, Jeff and the others retreated to the wagons and dropped down behind the wheels, pushing their rifles between the spokes.

"Watch both sides," Jeff warned.

He was not convinced that this was an Indian attack.

They were not out of farming country; it was no place for an Indian raid on wagons. Then he got a better look at the riders as they came closer in the dim light. They were painted something like Indians but their horses had saddles. It wasn't uncommon for Indians to have saddles any more but the renegade war parties seldom used them. They rode as Indians had done for the last hundred years and could hang on the far side of a running horse with only a leg and arm showing. These riders showed none of those characteristics.

The attack was real enough, however. The riders were firing their rifles with lethal intent but deplorable accuracy. In the dim light the answering shots from the wagons missed their targets, too, but it had the effect of making the riders swerve in a big arc and gallop back out of range.

"They sure don't act nothing like Indians," Beany grunted. "Real Indians would have circled and poured lead and arrows into our back sides."

Jeff agreed. With only three wagons, the best he could do for protection was to keep the wagons close together. Three wagons wouldn't make much of a circle. Indians bent on overrunning the camp would have been quick to take advantage of the exposed rear of the defenders.

"Looks like they're going to try to sneak in on foot," Norrie said when the raiders dismounted well beyond rifle range. "We can fight them off, can't we?"

"I think so," Jeff said. "They should do better with their rifles from the ground, though, than they did on horseback. If they circle, we'll have more trouble.

Terpko, you and Norrie stay here under the front wagon. Beany, you and I will take the back wagon."

"What about the middle wagon?" Terpko asked.

"I figure Bessie and the girls can handle that area."

Jeff got up and scooted back to the rear of the middle wagon. Poking his head under the canvas top, he looked around. It was too dark to see much but he did see that each girl held a rifle.

"Are the varmints sneaking in?" Bessie asked, peering out through the front opening over the seat of the wagon.

"Looks like it," Jeff said. "Can you keep them away from this wagon?"

"You can bank on us," Bessie said. "But we can't do much cooped up in here. Outside, girls, and under the wagon." She looked at Jeff. "We may not win any prizes for accuracy but we'll come close enough to put bees in their bonnets."

Jeff backed off to the rear wagon. Those riflemen would be within range soon. Jeff was willing to bet that Ivie was the leader. He wondered where he got the men to help him in the fight. They likely hadn't expected a great deal of resistance. If it was Posey that Ivie was after, he might have expected to hit the wagons, grab Posey, and escape in one quick strike. He knew now that it wasn't going to be that easy.

The rifles opened up out in the grass. The pale dawn was growing brighter but there was enough grass out there to hide a man lying prone. All the defenders had to fire at were the heads that suddenly popped up to fire a rifle.

Jeff shot at every available target, stealing glances now and then at Terpko and the girls. Terpko was firing steadily but it seemed to Jeff that it was always when there were no targets to aim at. He remembered the earnest conversation that Terpko had had with Ivie before the gambler had left the camp the other night.

It was a different situation under the middle wagon. The girls were squeezed in behind the wheels, three girls using the front wheel for cover; two girls and Bessie using the rear wheel. Bessie herself was more than that wheel would protect, Jeff thought.

But their fire was steady and aimed only where a head bobbed up. Jeff couldn't tell how accurate it was but there was no doubt about the intent. His admiration for the girls rose sharply as he watched them.

The riflemen in the grass were coming closer with their shots. Jeff yelled over to Bessie.

"Send a couple of the girls over here. More room behind these wheels."

Posey and Lily immediately started wriggling toward the rear wagon. Jeff squatted behind the front wheel, his rifle ready. He fired at every movement, keeping the raiders pinned down.

Posey stopped at the wheel beside Jeff. She poked her rifle barrel between the spokes and waited grimly. She was still afraid but not so much that it was interfering with her concentration.

"Like to get a bead on Ivie?" he asked.

She shot him a quick look then turned back to the prairie. "I would," she said.

He glanced over at Lily. She had been the one most

frightened by Ivie's tales of Indian raids. She was still frightened but in dead earnest about her shooting. Over under the middle wagon, Jeff could see from the way Bessie handled a gun that she was no stranger to one. Her shots were not being wasted, he was sure.

The raiders halted some distance from the wagons. After a ten minute exchange of shots at a range that required pure luck to be effective, they began a slow retreat. Jeff guessed that Ivie's hired gunmen had had enough of trying to overrun the wagons, supposedly defended by helpless women.

"We did it!" Beany yelled. "We showed the ding-busted varmints! Shall we run them into the river?"

"Let's let well enough alone," Jeff said. "Anybody hit?"

"Toni got a splinter in her neck when a bullet nicked a wagon spoke," Bessie said.

Jeff crawled over to the wagon, not sure yet that all the raiders had retreated. Bessie had the splinter out when he got there but the wound was seeping a little blood.

"When did that happen?" he said.

"Quite a while ago," Toni said.

"She didn't let me know," Bessie said. "Just kept on shooting."

"I'd rather have a splinter than to lose my hair," Toni said. "Will they come back?"

"I doubt it," Jeff said. "I think they've had enough."

Jeff crawled out from under the wagon and studied the prairie. The men mounting their horses well out of rifles range. He called for breakfast to start.

The girls moved out to their regular jobs. He especially admired Toni. Not many girls would stay with a battle after being punctured by a splinter. All the girls did well, even Lily, who had been so scared. Only Terpko left a suspicion in Jeff's mind. He had fired his rifle often enough but Jeff doubted if he had intended to hit anything.

The wagons moved out, losing only an hour due to the dawn raid. At noon, they went hungry because of Hercules. Bessie had finished cooking the stew and set the iron kettle on the ground while she got the pans. The billy goat trotted to the unattended pot and stuck his nose into it. It was hot and he bleated wildly as he reared back. But the bail of the iron kettle caught on a horn and he upset the kettle as he retreated.

With the kettle dangling from a horn and dragging on the ground, the goat backed away faster and faster, bleating in terror. Bessie saw what was happening and took after the runaway kettle and goat, screaming curses that she would have castigated Beany for using. Fifty yards from the wagons, the kettle bail came off the goat's horn and he ran free, retreating until he was sure he was safe, both from the kettle and Bessie's wrath.

Star went after the goat while Bessie screamed that she would slice him into pieces the size of a gnat's heel if she ever caught him.

"You won't get a chance if I get to him first," Beany yelled. "He ruined all our dinner."

"You won't get anything else till supper, either," Bessie promised.

Jeff ordered the wagons on. They had lost enough time already.

For supper, Bessie insisted that Posey do most of the cooking since she had said she was a cook. Jeff was sure that if everyone hadn't been so hungry from missing the noon meal, the supper would have gone uneaten.

Jeff caught Terpko beyond the wagons just at dusk teasing Hercules. He held up his neckerchief, waving it wildly. Hercules couldn't resist charging at it. Terpko would jerk the flag away and laugh at the goat. Jeff was just ready to shout at Terpko when Star ran past him.

"Stop that!" she yelled. "You'll make him mean."

"Wave Terpko a while and let that goat butt him," Beany said. "Anyway, he can't make that son of Satan mean. He was born that way."

It was a hot night and even the girls brought their bedrolls out of the wagon and spread them on the ground. Jeff had just roused in the early dawn light and was thinking of getting up when he heard someone slipping over to him. Turning his head, he recognized Star.

"What's wrong?" he asked softly, lounging up on an elbow.

"There's a rattlesnake on Toni. His head is only a foot from her face."

A chill ran through Jeff. If Toni made a move, that snake would strike. She wouldn't have a chance.

V

Jeff grabbed his revolver which he kept in his blankets each night. Moving quietly toward the center wagon where the girls were sleeping under and around the wagon, he followed Star's pointing finger toward the one near the front wheel.

One set of blankets was empty. That would be Star's bed. Then he was close enough to see the huge rattler on Toni's blankets, only inches from her head. Jeff looked quickly at Toni's face to see if the snake had already bitten her and if she was dead. But her eyes were open wide and rolling toward him.

"Don't move a muscle," Jeff said softly. "Keep breathing as normal as you can."

"The others are still asleep," Star whispered. "I was afraid to wake them. They might panic and scare the snake."

Jeff nodded. "Good thinking."

He moved closer to Toni. He had to kill the snake before it could bite her and he had to do it without hurting her if possible. He was amazed at her control. He doubted if he could lie that still if he had a rattler on his chest.

When he was within a few feet of Toni, the snake stirred, turning its attention from Toni's face to the direction of Jeff. Jeff had heard that a snake always faced any movement that held heat. The sensors in the pits between its eyes and nostrils caught the heat.

Slowly he cocked the revolver and began extending his arm toward the snake. The snake followed the movement unerringly.

"Don't move," he whispered again to Toni.

With the gun held steady, Jeff pushed it toward the snake. The snake faced it and when the muzzle was only inches from its head, Jeff squeezed the trigger. The head of the snake snapped off as if a knife had cut it.

Jeff felt the tension explode in him. But the next instant he found himself in the middle of an uproar. Everyone in camp, violently awakened by the gun, was screaming or roaring questions.

Toni erupted out of her blankets as if they were on fire. Bessie began bellowing like a blind bull, trying to find out what had happened. Beany was clawing for his gun, yelling, "Indians! Turn out!"

Star was holding Toni, who was sobbing now. She explained to Bessie and the other girls what had happened. Jeff turned away, feeling weak and almost sick. Toni couldn't have been much closer to death. She was so small and that snake was a big one. A bite from him would surely have carried enough venom to have killed her.

Jeff went about the morning chores, still a little shaken but thoroughly impressed by the courage Toni had shown. A snake gave him the shivers. He was sure Toni must share those feelings; at least, after this experience.

The excitement died down except for one explosion when Bessie, finishing the breakfast, tossed salt over her left shoulder to ward off bad luck and hit Beany right in the face with it.

"Ding-bust it, woman!" Beany roared, wiping the salt out of one eye. "You ain't got the sense of a louse!"

Bessie scowled at Beany. "That was to keep away bad luck. And I'd say you were about as bad luck as a body can find."

"I'll show you what bad luck is if you pull a stunt like that again," Beany retorted, still rubbing his eye.

The wagons got moving a little earlier than usual, due to the camp having been suddenly catapulted into day when Jeff shot the snake. Jeff moved out in front of the wagons to scout, not expecting trouble but thinking he might find an easier crossing of some of the gullies where the tracks of the old trail had worn such deep ruts. He was aware of another rider coming from the wagons before he had gone far. He twisted in the saddle to see Lily riding toward him, mounted on one of the extra horses Beany had brought along.

"Mind if I ride with you?" Lily asked, reining up beside him. "It gets boring riding with the girls all day."

Jeff shrugged. "Probably good for the saddle horses to get a little work, too, instead of trailing along behind the wagons day after day."

"I thought so." She paused. "That was a brave thing you did this morning, killing that snake and saving Toni."

"Toni was the brave one," Jeff corrected. "If she'd panicked and made a sudden move, the snake would have struck."

"She pretends to go into a trance sometimes to talk to spirits. Maybe that's why she could hold so still. You saved her from drowning, too. I doubt if she realizes how much she owes you."

"She doesn't owe me anything," Jeff said. "It's my job as wagon boss."

"Nothing ever happens to me," Lily said plaintively.

Jeff shot a quick glance at her. Lily was the tall one; that was really all he had noticed about her. She was taller than everyone with the wagons except Jeff and Terpko and she was only about an inch shorter than either of them. Jeff was surprised at her sudden interest in him but realized, when he considered it, that he shouldn't have been. Lily was going west to get married and, like most girls, wanted a man taller than she was. At her height, almost six feet, her choices were limited. Jeff apparently didn't look like too bad a catch to her so why should she wait till she got to Colorado and take a chance on what she would get?

"You're lucky if nothing happens to you like it has to Toni," he said.

Lily shook her head. "Toni's the lucky one. She got all the attention and is none the worse for what has happened."

"Your good luck will come when you get to Colorado," Jeff said.

Lily rode with him for half an hour then went back to the wagons. He looked after her, thinking that maybe he was a fool for not responding to her obvious advance. She was nice looking and he guessed she was a pretty nice girl. She was older than some of the others. Twenty-five, Beany said. But Jeff was twenty-eight.

He was on this trip to guide these girls to Colorado, not to pick one himself, he thought. But if there *was* one—well, it wouldn't be Lily.

The train settled into a routine that became more efficient as it moved west. Trouble faded to a murmur. Even Hercules behaved himself for several days. The wagons reached Salina and moved on toward Fort Harker. From there west, the danger would increase. Jeff had heard that the Kansas Pacific Railroad would reach Denver this summer. For almost five years now, The Butterfield Overland Despatch stage coaches had run from the end of track to Denver. When the rails reached Denver, the B. O. D. would be no more.

Jeff was going to follow the old B. O. D. trail. The newspaper said there was no danger from Indians any longer. But from what Jeff had heard from freighters returning from the west and what he knew of Indians, he didn't believe that all the danger was past.

Jeff's sense of uneasiness took a sharp rise one night when he happened to wake up just as Terpko, who was standing guard, moved farther out from the wagons than he had been posted. Jeff followed cautiously. It was too dark to see where Terpko went. His suspicions soared and he watched until Terpko came back and took up his post again.

The next evening, he announced that two men at a time would stand guard during the night. Doubling the guard, he told himself, would prevent Terpko from slipping away and meeting someone beyond the limits of the camp. Jeff could think of no other reason for his leaving his post.

His announcement of doubling the guard brought a storm of fearful questions. He tried to make it plain that he didn't expect any trouble. They weren't in Indian country yet, wouldn't be until they passed Fort Harker. It was just a precaution. But he wasn't sure that he convinced anyone.

They camped for the night close to a creek with some fairly tall chalk bluffs. Samson flushed a rabbit and chased it along the foot of the bluffs. Beany dropped his camp chores and ran after the dog and rabbit, yelling that they would have rabbit stew for supper.

It was several minutes before Beany appeared again at the foot of the bluff, fifty yards from the camp. While only a few people in camp could see Beany when he first appeared, there wasn't anyone who wasn't fully aware of his approach.

Bessie jerked up her head like a startled grizzly. "What in blazes?" she roared, sniffing the air. Then she spotted Beany stamping angrily toward camp. "Hold it!" she bellowed. "Don't you come a step closer!"

Jeff was at the side of the wagons now facing Beany. "What kind of a rabbit were you chasing?" he demanded, wrinkling his nose.

Beany stopped a few yards away. "Samson ran that rabbit into a hole down there," he explained. "Only trouble was, the hole we thought he went into was the wrong one. Samson backed out howling with a skunk right after him."

"You didn't have to pet the varmint," Bessie roared. "You stay out of camp till you smell decent."

"I'll starve to death before that," Beany complained.

"Where's Samson?" one of the girls asked.

"He probably went to the creek for a bath," Bessie said. "Which ain't a bad idea." She scowled at Beany.

"I'll get some other clothes and go to the creek, too," Beany said.

Bessie shook her head. "No, you don't. You ain't going to get that stink off with plain cold water. You're going to take a bath with plenty of soap."

"The creek will wash the soap away," Beany complained.

"Reckon it would," Bessie said. "So you can scrub up in our bath tent."

Beany howled like a dog with his tail in a trap. "I ain't taking no bath in no woman's bathtub," he yelled.

"You sure ain't," Bessie agreed. "You can use the old wash tub we have. Then you take it to the creek and scrub it out. But you're going to take a bath with plenty of soap. I ain't going to travel with no second-hand skunk."

The girls already had the bath tent set up. They used it almost every night when they were camped close enough to a creek to get water easily. Bessie usually kept a fire going after supper to heat water for the little tub in the tent.

Now she put water onto heat before the supper went into the pots. Jeff and Norrie carried water up from the creek and Bessie heated some while the rest was taken into the tent and poured into the little wash tub that

Bessie had put there. She set a big bar of home-made soap next to the tub. When the water on the fire was hot, she carried it in and poured it into the tub, heating that water to a luke-warm degree.

Stepping outside the tent, she bellowed for Beany to come on into camp and get his bath. The girls were clustered behind their wagon, giggling like school girls as they watched Beany come stamping into camp, grumbling with every step.

"Ding-bust it!" he muttered. "It would wear off if you'd give it time."

"It's bad enough having you act like a bee-stung bull," Bessie snapped. "We don't have to put up with you smelling like a skunk, too."

Beany disappeared into the tent where he was soon splashing around like a walrus in a wash bowl. Bessie bawled instructions to him from the supper fire and the girls giggled. It was that giggling that was really upsetting Beany, Jeff guessed. It must be pretty disconcerting to a man who had lived without women for forty years to have those girls making fun of his predicament. Jeff didn't expect Beany to take any longer with his bath than he absolutely had to.

Samson came into camp, soaking wet from his swim in the creek. Jeff guessed he smelled stronger than Beany but there was no way to tell. Everyone had his nose full of the aroma of skunk now and the added incense that Samson brought in went unnoticed.

Dusk gathered quickly as Bessie got the supper ready. No one seemed to have much appetite. Jeff expected Beany to come out of the tent before long but he didn't. Then he realized he was waiting to sneak out after it got dark.

Then just as darkness had turned objects out on the prairie into obscure bumps and hollows, Terpko came running back toward the wagons from the spot where he had been watching the surrounding area.

"Indians!" he shouted. "A whole passel of them heading this way."

Jeff leaped for the wagon and got his rifle. Peering out into the deepening darkness, he tried to locate the Indians. He saw a small herd of what he took to be antelope loping away across the prairie. But he saw no Indians. Instantly, he realized that if antelope were out there, Indians weren't. Wild game wouldn't stay near Indians. He was surprised that antelope were even this close to the wagons.

But just as he was about to announce that it was a false alarm, the tent flap jerked open and Beany charged out. He had the towel that Bessie had given him wrapped loosely around him but he was wearing nothing else. He dashed for the wagon, grabbed a shotgun since no rifle was handy, and dropped down behind a wheel, shoving the gun barrel through the spokes.

"Where are the varmints?" he demanded.

Bessie and the girls were too shocked to say anything. They each held a rifle but they weren't looking for Indians. They were staring at Beany.

Even Samson seemed surprised at the sight of Beany without his clothes. The dog moved up behind Beany as if to make sure it was really him. He stuck out his nose and sniffed, likely surprised at the unfamiliar smell of soap on Beany. His cold wet nose touched a spot on Beany's hip not covered by the towel.

Beany's bellow would have made an elephant's trumpeting sound like a whisper. He lunged forward as if he thought an Indian was burning him with a firebrand. At the same moment, the shotgun roared as Beany's fingers clamped down on both triggers. His head connected solidly with the hub of the wagon wheel and he dropped to the ground as if he had been shot.

"Did somebody kill him?" one of the girls asked in the total silence that followed the explosion.

"He probably broke the wagon wheel," Bessie said.

But she was moving swiftly toward Beany. Jeff was running that way, too. The girls were staring at Beany but Posey reminded them of their primary purpose, defending themselves against an Indian attack. Jeff thought of telling them it was a false alarm but his concern at the moment was for Beany.

Dropping on one knee, he felt for a pulse in Beany's wrist. It was there, strong and steady. "Must have just knocked himself out," Jeff said.

"Should have known you couldn't hurt him by hitting him on the head," Bessie said. "Him and that goat would make a real good butting contest."

"We'd better put him in a wagon till he comes to," Jeff suggested.

"And get some clothes on him," Bessie said, adjusting the towel over him. "He ain't pretty with clothes on. He's a sight worse without them."

Bessie grabbed his arms and Jeff took his feet and they started toward the rear of the back wagon. Beany began stirring and Jeff was going to suggest they lay him down because he was reviving without help. But at that moment, Hercules came around the corner of the wagon, saw Bessie backing toward him, and stopped, shaking his head and bleating.

Bessie heard the bleat and promptly forgot her humanitarian impulses. She dropped Beany and whirled to face the enemy. Hercules backed off. Beany, who had been coming out of his fog, hit the ground with a thud. That seemed to revive him and he jerked free of Jeff and came to his feet, sputtering like a wet candle.

Clutching the towel around him, he stared at Bessie then at the girls who had forgotten the Indians again and were watching developments at the rear wagon.

"What in ding-busted tarnation are you doing?" he screamed at Bessie. "Lugging me around like a side of beef!"

Bessie, having squelched Hercules' desire to get into the act, wheeled on Beany. "I'd a sight rather lug a side of beef around than something that looks and smells like an over-sized skinned skunk."

Beany glanced around again then headed on a run for the tent where he had his fresh clothes ready to put on. Hercules, seeing the corner of the towel waving behind Beany, gave immediate chase. Beany slammed through the flap of the tent just a jump ahead of Hercules. The goat, seeing his target disappear, slid to a halt a foot from the tent.

"I'll kill that ding-busted goat and every female on this train!" Beany squalled from inside the tent.

"How?" Bessie yelled back. "Talk us to death? You even came out second best with a polecat."

It took the camp an extra hour to settle down that night. The skunk odor permeated every corner of the camp and only the soft night breeze made life tolerable. Jeff switched Beany's and Norrie's turn at guard, putting Norrie with Terpko for the first shift.

It was a half hour before Jeff and Beany were scheduled to take over as guard when Beany slipped over to Jeff's bed under the lead wagon. It was the mixed odor of skunk and strong soap that wakened Jeff before Beany reached him.

"There's someone sneaking into the back wagon," Beany whispered. "Might be an Indian."

Jeff came full awake. "Let's get him!"

VI

Jeff was out of his blankets in an instant with his gun in his hand. Before he got out of the deep shadow of the wagon, however, he saw someone moving next to the middle wagon. He recognized Bessie.

"What bit her?" Beany whispered.

"Probably saw the same thing you saw," Jeff said softly. "She's closer. She's going to get there first."

"Poor guy!" Beany muttered. "The worst we'd do would be shoot him."

Jeff and Beany moved out where they could see

what Bessie was doing and be ready to help if she did tackle the burglar. For the first time, Jeff got a glimpse of the thief. He was standing at the back of the wagon with his head and shoulders inside, apparently looking for something. Jeff couldn't imagine what. Only the trunks belonging to the girls and Bessie were in that wagon.

Bessie was moving quietly toward the rear wagon. She stopped dead still once, staring out beyond the last wagon at the prairie, lighted only by the stars. Jeff switched his eyes that way and saw the goat, Hercules, out there, watching the proceedings carefully. Star had picketed the two nanny goats where they could get some good grass. She never tied up Hercules but he usually stayed close to them.

"What's Bessie up to now?" Beany whispered.

"Don't know," Jeff said. "We'd better be ready to help her, whatever it is."

Bessie was moving silently along the side of the wagon, approaching the spot where the thief was still engrossed in what he was doing just inside the wagon. Bessie had taken off her nightcap, letting her hair fall down over her shoulders.

When she reached the back of the wagon, Jeff expected her to jump on the thief. But she made no quick move or sound. Instead, she held out the nightcap and began waving it directly behind the thief. Jeff knew then what she had in mind. He would never have thought to use Hercules to get the thief. He wondered suddenly how the thief had slipped past Norrie and Terpko to get into camp. He didn't wonder what was going to happen to him now if he didn't hear Hercules coming.

The goat shook his beard a time or two then lowered his head and charged. On the grass, his hoofs made little noise and the thief apparently was too busy at his task to notice.

He evidently got his first inkling that he was not alone just before the goat reached him. He jerked his head up but didn't have time to turn around before Hercules reached his target. There was a yell followed by a heavy grunt as the thief was boosted through the back opening of the wagon into the mass of trunks inside.

Jeff and Beany dashed for the wagon but Bessie was already around behind the wagon, kicking at the goat and blocking the exit for the thief. Jeff crowded in beside Bessie, his gun poking through the canvas opening.

"Know who it is?" he asked Bessie, trying to see inside. It was pitch black inside the canvas covered wagon among the trunks.

"Sure," Bessie said. "It's that sour-faced Terpko. Don't know what he's looking for but that billy goat came in handy for once in his rotten life."

"Come out of there," Jeff ordered, backing away a step but keeping the gun pointed inside.

"Put down the gun," Terpko said. "I ain't going to start no war."

"You already started one with that billy goat," Beany said.

Terpko climbed out of the wagon, his eye on the

goat instead of Jeff's gun.

"What were you doing in that wagon?" Jeff demanded.

Terpko only glared at Jeff. Bessie poked her head inside then jerked it out again. "He was pawing through Posey's trunk," she said. She pushed up against Terpko. "What's Posey got that you want?"

"Nothing," Terpko said. "I was standing guard when I heard something in that wagon. I figured it might be some varmint that we had picked up on the road and I was looking for it."

"Too bad it wasn't a rattler," Bessie snapped. She looked at Jeff. "Do you believe that story?"

"Pretty hard to swallow," Jeff said. "Why did you pick Posey's trunk to rummage through?"

"I heard a noise in that trunk," Terpko said sullenly.

"I've dreamed up better stories than that after eating Bessie's stew," Beany said. "You'd better try again."

Jeff was thinking furiously. They would be short-handed if he fired Terpko, which was his first impulse. If Terpko was gone, Jeff might not find out what he'd been looking for in Posey's trunk. Then another thought hit him. It had been just two nights ago that he'd seen Terpko slip away from camp. Had he met someone out there? Had that person ordered Terpko to find something in Posey's trunk? Jeff reached a sudden decision to keep Terpko under close watch for a while to see if he would contact his night visitor again. Jeff wanted to see that man more than he wanted to be rid of Terpko.

"I'll forget what I just saw," he said. "But if I catch

you near the girls' trunks again, you're through with this train. You can walk back from wherever we are."

"Let's tie him to the back of the wagon and lead him like a horse," Beany suggested. "I'll fasten a flag to his hip pocket and let the goat boost him along in case he gets tired."

Terpko scowled but he shot a nervous glance at the goat. Bessie grunted, obviously displeased with Jeff's decision.

"It ain't often that I agree with Beany," she said. "But this time I think he's got a good idea."

Terpko hurried back to his post before Beany and Bessie decided to take things into their own hands. Jeff doubted if he'd have any more trouble with Terpko tonight. But his suspicions of the big driver had come to a head. There had to be a showdown soon.

Jeff and Beany took over the guard duties at midnight and came back into camp when the dawn light was bright enough that the surrounding prairie was clearly visible. The camp was stirring. Bessie had the breakfast cooking and the girls were arranging things in the wagons for the day's travel.

Jeff called Posey to one side. "We found Terpko digging into your trunk last night," he said. "Do you have anything in there that he might want?"

Surprise showed in her face. Evidently Bessie hadn't told the girls about Terpko's prowling and they hadn't investigated his yell. She quickly recovered and shook her head.

"There's nothing in there but clothes. He would hardly want them."

Jeff wasn't sure whether to believe her or not. He wished he could see in the trunk but he wasn't going to snoop.

"I wish he wasn't here," Posey added. "I'm almost afraid of him."

"If he gets out of line again, he won't be here," Jeff said.

Before they moved the wagons, Jeff suggested to Star that she might tie up her goat. He wasn't the least bit selective in his targets when he was in a butting mood. His suggestion made no impression, he could see.

Star did, however, saddle a horse and ride out in front of the wagons where Jeff was checking their course. She reined in beside him.

"Hercules is my watch dog," she explained. "He will protect me as well as any dog will guard anybody. Do you hate goats that much?"

"Can't recall that I said I hated goats," Jeff said. "I just don't care much for the manners of this one."

Star watched him for so long that he began to feel uncomfortable. She was sizing him up as if she had never seen him before. She wasn't far from Jeff's age. Beany had said she made no bones about searching for a husband. Jeff suddenly felt that he was being evaluated for the job right now. Her next words seemed to confirm that suspicion.

"If I had someone to protect me, I wouldn't need Hercules."

"When you get to Colorado and find your cowboy, he isn't likely to take the billy goat in the deal," he said. "Cowboys like cattle but have little use for sheep and even less for goats."

"You don't have much use for women, either, do you?"

"I've never had much chance to like them," Jeff said. "There were usually a few girls in the wagon trains I guided but for every single girl in a train, there seemed to be at least a half dozen single young men and that usually meant trouble."

"It's different here," Star said.

"I'm not sure this isn't worse," Jeff said.

Star smiled. "Maybe you're just a woman hater."

Jeff didn't know what to say to that. He didn't say anything because at that moment, he saw something beside the trail ahead. He lifted himself in the stirrups for a better view and Star followed his example.

"Could be a dead animal," Jeff said cautiously. "Or a man. Or an Indian lying in ambush. You'd better get back to the wagons while I find out what it is." He nudged his horse forward.

"Maybe I can do something to help," Star said and kept pace with him.

Jeff didn't object. He had already identified the lump beside the road as a man. From his clothes, he guessed he wasn't an Indian. Anyway, there was no hiding place close by from which an ambush could be sprung.

Spurring his horse forward, Jeff reined up beside the man. The man rolled over and sat up, staring at Jeff and Star. Jeff swung down.

"What's wrong, fellow?"

"I'm lost, afoot, and starved," the man said.

"What are you doing out here?" Jeff helped the man to his feet. He was of average size with piercing, slate colored eyes.

"Four of us started to Denver," the man said. "We took nothing but food and bedrolls. Couldn't afford the train. Somewhere, not far west of Fort Harker, we were jumped by Indians. Terrible fight. I was the only one who got away. They wounded my horse and he finally gave out on me. I've been wandering ever since."

"You poor man," Star exclaimed. "We've got plenty of food."

"Won't take long for the wagons to get here," Jeff said. "We'll stop long enough to feed him."

Star went back to meet the wagons. Jeff turned his attention to the man again. He didn't look starved nor did his clothes look as if he'd been walking over the prairie for any length of time. The gun on his hip caught Jeff's eye. The holster was tied down and the handle of the gun had seen plenty of use.

"Like the gun?" the man asked. "You're probably wondering why I'm wearing it. If I wasn't good with a gun, I wouldn't be here now. The other three with me were not as good. One was my brother."

"What were you going to do in Denver?" Jeff asked.

"I'm a gambler," the man said simply. "My brother and the other men were merchants. They hoped to get started in business."

Jeff frowned. "Merchants going to Denver without anything to sell?"

The man shrugged. "Opportunities show up if a man

gets to the place where they are. We figured to make out all right."

Just before the wagons reached them, Jeff asked, "Do you have a name?"

"Vinton Zorn," the man said. "I sure appreciate your hospitality."

The wagons stopped and Star and the other girls quickly got food for Zorn. Star had obviously spread the word about the stranger. Even Bessie came hurrying forward with food. She looked Zorn over with a far more critical eye, however, than did the girls.

While he ate, Zorn recounted in detail his fight with the Indians and his miraculous escape. The girls listened in awe, obviously believing every word. Even Beany listened raptly. Zorn relished the attention.

"He's a lucky fellow," Beany said to Jeff.

"Right now he is," Jeff said. "I suppose you'd like to have all those girls fussing over you?"

Beany jerked his eyes away from Zorn and the girls and shook his head. "I don't want any women wooling me around. I mean he's lucky to get out of that scrape alive."

"Does he look to you like he'd been wandering around the prairie for days without anything to eat?" Jeff asked. "His clothes don't have a tear—they're not even very dirty. And he's not eating like a starving man."

Beany frowned. "You're right. He ain't starving. A man gets hungry enough, even pretty girls don't take his mind off grub."

"He says he's a gambler," Jeff said. "He may be

gambling on something right now. He'll do to watch."

"Reckon so," Beany agreed soberly.

Jeff expected the man to go as far as Fort Harker where he could get a horse to return east. But they passed the fort and Zorn was still with them. Terpko seemed to get along better with Zorn that with anyone in the train.

"Thought you'd get a horse and head back home," Jeff said to Zorn as they left the fort.

"Why should I," Zorn asked easily, "unless you're kicking me out? I was headed for Denver. I'll pay you for your trouble and the food I eat as soon as I get set up in Denver. Won't take me long to make that much in a mining town."

"We don't go all the way to Denver. And we travel slow. You were traveling fast."

"And I'm the only one still traveling," Zorn said. "I feel safer in a crowd."

"If you're going to travel with us, then you can take your turn at guard duty," Jeff said. "We're west of Fort Harker now. From here on, we might see some Indians."

Zorn nodded. "You can bet on it. We did."

Jeff watched Zorn's actions around camp. He could find little fault with the gambler except his overtures to the girls. Posey brushed him off, branding him a two-bit gambler. The others gathered around him to hear the stories he told about his adventures since leaving the Missouri River on the way to Denver. Cheery seemed especially fascinated by the man and his stories.

"He'd have to have been on the road for two years to have all that happen to him," Beany said to Jeff one night after listening to Zorn's tales.

"I'm guessing he was out here only long enough to get lost and be found by us," Jeff said. "I'm wondering if it just happened to be us who found him or if that was one of his sure bets."

A few nights out of Fort Harker, Zorn's stories of the Indians got some bolstering. Bessie had already begun doubting everything the gambler said. The girls still believed it all, even when he had a new story for them every night.

They were just ready for supper when Norrie, who was watching, pointed excitedly to five riders coming toward them in the dusk. Jeff moved to the front wagon to watch them. Behind them was the bright sky where the sun had set and it wasn't until they were fairly close that he positively identified them as Indians.

"They're peaceful," he said to the others. "They wouldn't be riding in like that unless they just wanted to talk."

Jeff moved out from the wagons to meet them. They pulled up their horses and the leader held up a hand in a sign of greeting.

"Want food, whisky," he said in understandable English.

Jeff nodded. "Food, yes. No whisky in these wagons."

The Indians slid off their ponies. Jeff turned to Bessie who obviously didn't approve of letting the Indians come into the camp. Jeff would have preferred making them ride on. But there were five of them, and while the men in the train might win in the battle, somebody would be killed and there were likely many more Indians not far away.

"Feed them," Jeff said to Bessie.

The Indians sat down, cross-legged, and waited to be served. They had been uninvited guests at camps like this before, Jeff saw. Likely they were trail beggars.

But their black eyes brightened when they saw the girls around the fire. Jeff didn't like that. Women were one thing the Indians knew they couldn't get for the asking. But that was the grand prize every warrior wanted. It made him a big man in his camp.

Jeff kept his hand on his gun as he watched. Would they try to take the girls with them now? He would rather they'd do that and bring about a showdown right here while he and Beany were alert than to try a sneak attack later to steal the girls.

Jeff didn't know which to expect but he did know that the looks in those Indians' eyes meant real trouble.

VII

Bessie was slow in getting the food to the Indians. They glared at her but she motioned the girls back to the wagon while she went over to talk to Jeff.

"Can they understand me?" she asked softly.

"Maybe," Jeff said. "One of them can speak English. Better feed them before they decide to scalp us."

Bessie glowered at the five Indians. "There ain't as

71

many of them as there are of us. But I'll feed them. Just keep them busy till I get the supper ready."

"Thought it was ready," Jeff said.

"It ain't," Bessie said sharply and turned to the front wagon where the provisions were kept.

Jeff moved over to the Indian who had acted as spokesman before. "The cook will make special supper for you," he said.

The Indian nodded but the frown on his face told Jeff he didn't like to wait. Jeff turned to hurry Bessie but she was already coming toward the campfire. She stirred the stew that she had cooked for their own supper and then, sniffing it, she nodded and started dipping it up into tin plates.

"Who's the hungriest?" Bessie demanded, taking the first plate toward the row of seated Indians.

"Me good Indian," the spokesman said.

Bessie nodded and handed him the plate. "Slop it down," she said, "then get out of here so we can get some sleep."

Jeff frowned as he watched Bessie. She wasn't acting like he had expected her to in the face of danger. He wouldn't believe that she didn't recognize the danger, especially since the Indians had seen the five young women with the wagons.

Bessie gave plates to the other Indians and they began eating with a relish that suggested they were really hungry.

Terpko moved over to the campfire while the Indians were engrossed in their supper. He peeked into the kettle then turned to get a plate.

"We might as well get our supper, too," he said.

Bessie stepped between him and the kettle. "Our guests eat first," she snapped.

Terpko frowned. "Maybe you call them guests; I call them beggars."

"They eat first," Bessie said firmly. "You'll wait with the rest of us. There ain't enough left for all of us so we'll all wait and eat together."

"Just who do you think you are, bossing everybody around?" Terpko snapped, pushing against Bessie.

The Indians stopped eating to watch the argument. Likely they had never seen a woman stand up to a man before.

"I'm the cook, that's who," Bessie said. "If you ain't careful, you'll get a fork rammed down your throat."

"I ain't so sure she wouldn't do it," Zorn said from the side of the wagon where he had been watching the Indians.

"Her cooking ain't worth fighting over," Terpko said and turned away, scowling at the Indians and Bessie with equal animosity.

The Indians finished their supper and got up. They stared at the girls, aware now that two of them were holding rifles. Then with a grunt, they turned to their ponies and rode back to the west, the way they had come.

"I don't like it, Jeff," Beany said when they were gone.

"That makes at least two of us," Jeff said. "I wish they hadn't seen the girls. We'll have to keep a sharp lookout every minute from here on."

73

"Should have shot the whole bunch," Zorn said. "We had enough rifles to do it. You don't let the other fellow take a high scoring trick if you've got a bigger trump."

"They held the ace, Zorn," Jeff said. "There are plenty more where they came from. If we'd killed them, the whole war party would have been on us before morning."

"Hey!" Terpko yelled at Bessie and Jeff wheeled to see Bessie emptying the stew on the ground.

"You can make me wait," Terpko roared, "but making me go without is too much even for a proddy old heifer like you."

"You watch your tongue, mister," Bessie said, wheeling on Terpko, "or you won't get any of the next batch I mix up, either."

"What was wrong with that stew?" Jeff asked, a light dawning.

"It had a big dose of calomel in it," Bessie said. "I'd have used strychnine if I'd had it."

"What will calomel do to them?" Norrie asked.

"Keep them busy for a day or two, anyway," Bessie said. "I put in a good dose. It doesn't have any taste and it doesn't smell but it's got more power than salts."

Terpko stared at Bessie. "That's why you wouldn't let me have any?"

"That's it, buster. I should have let you have some. That would have taken some of the ginger out of you."

"And everything else," Beany added. "Got to hand it to you, Bessie. You did something to keep them redskins off our backs for a while and the rest of us didn't do anything."

"I had the chance," Bessie said. "You didn't. But they may figure I did something to that stew and send their buddies back for our scalps."

"We'll increase the guard," Jeff said.

"We girls will take our turns, too," Toni said. "We've got as much reason to fight those dirty savages as you have."

"Reckon you can't argue with that," Bessie said to Jeff.

"You girls can help watch but you'll do it from your wagon," Jeff said. "We'll stand guard a ways outside camp. Under no circumstances do you leave the wagons."

"I'll see to that," Bessie said. "How are you going to increase the guard with only five of you?"

"Shorter hitches. We'll be more alert. Terpko and I will take the first watch, Beany and Norrie the second, and Zorn and I will take the last one."

"Hey," Zorn said, "that will be the dawn watch. That's when Indians usually attack."

"According to your stories, you've had lots of experience fighting Indians," Jeff said. "That's why I picked you for that time."

Zorn looked at the girls and didn't say any more but Jeff could imagine his face had turned a few shades lighter. Jeff had his reasons for standing watch with both Terpko and Zorn. He didn't trust either one. He'd be watching them as well as scanning the night for Indians.

Jeff didn't expect a return visit from the Indians tonight after hearing what Bessie had done. Maybe in a few days the Indians would find them again. They would be 'plenty mad' Indians then instead of 'plenty good' Indians.

He was amused at the relief in Zorn when dawn lightened the plains the next morning and there were no Indians. After getting his breakfast plate filled, Terpko followed Toni over to the middle wagon where he squatted down beside her as she sat on the wagon tongue to eat.

"Showed a lot of spunk to volunteer to stand guard last night," he said.

Jeff couldn't hear what she replied but a strange feeling began boiling up in the pit of his stomach and almost filled it so he couldn't swallow his breakfast. He watched Terpko and Toni, scowling as he watched, trying not to listen since what they said was none of his business.

"That's galling you a bit, ain't it?" Beany said softly at Jeff's side.

Jeff wheeled around to face Beany. "What do you mean?"

"I ain't blind even if I am old," Beany said. "You don't like Terpko and I don't blame you. But I'll bet he wouldn't be raising a blister under your saddle if he was talking to any of the other girls."

Jeff scowled. "What difference does it make which girl he talks to?"

Beany shrugged. "It doesn't to me. But it sure does to you. I've seen you sneaking looks at Toni. Can't say that I blame you. She's a mighty cute little filly."

"I'm taking these girls to Uncle Abe's cowboys, not

76

marrying them," Jeff said sharply.

"Sure, sure," Beany said. "But tell that to Terpko, not me."

Jeff finished his breakfast, not tasting a mouthful of it. This strange fury wasn't burning inside him because Terpko was singling out Toni to talk to, he told himself. It was because Jeff didn't trust the man and he didn't want any of the girls to have anything to do with him.

While they were hitching up the teams, Jeff made it a point to pass near Terpko. "You're hired to drive a team, not talk to the girls," he said softly.

Terpko jerked up his head. "Who I talk to is none of your business," he snapped.

"It's my business as long as I'm bossing these wagons," Jeff said. "You drive and I'll guide and the girls will be left alone. That clear?"

Terpko didn't say any more but he stared angrily at Jeff. Jeff rode on, taking his place out in front of the wagons. He was still seething inside.

He hoped that Terpko would obey his order to stay away from the girls but he really didn't expect him to. There was a stubborn streak in Terpko and he was a bully, the kind he was going to get in his way if he persisted in pressing his attention on Toni. He didn't know what would happen then but he'd find out.

Terpko kept away from the girls at camp that night. Beany took the extra shift in guard duty, standing watch with Terpko in the early hours and with Norrie during the hours before dawn. That left Jeff and Zorn to handle the midnight shift. Jeff appreciated the reprieve. He knew that neither of them could take guard duty two thirds of every night and still do his work during the day.

Jeff put Beany in the front wagon for a couple of hours to nap as best he could while the wagon jolted over the prairie. In the afternoon, he took the same privilege while Beany rode well out in front to scout. Jeff didn't expect to sleep but he knew he needed rest.

He was surprised when he woke up later to find that he had gone sound asleep in spite of the jolting of the wagon. He mounted and rode out in front, checking with Beany on his mule, Angel, then started to look for a good camping site. He found what he was looking for at the abandoned Butterfield Overland Despatch station on Big Creek. They had passed Old Fort Fletcher early this morning. It had been abandoned after the disastrous flood of 1867 in favor of the new Fort Hays, several miles up Big Creek.

"We should be safe enough here," Jeff said to Beany as they pulled the wagons up for camp. "We're not too far from Fort Hays."

"Those redskins have had time enough now to get over the calomel," Beany said doubtfully. "I don't trust them."

"Who does?" He looked over the area. "We'll camp close to the station."

The Indians were pushed out of Jeff's mind at supper. Terpko took his plate and deliberately marched over to squat beside Toni again. His eyes flipped challengingly toward Jeff. Jeff sat his plate aside.

"Start off by hitting him over the head with a neckyoke," Beany said softly.

"Might not be a bad idea," Jeff agreed.

"You've got to win, you know, or you won't be bossing the train any more."

Jeff nodded. This wasn't the first time authority had been challenged as boss of a wagon train. But this was the first time he had been in a fight over a girl.

Jeff moved toward the area where the girls were eating. There was concern in their faces as they watched him coming. Terpko had turned his attention to Toni and she was talking to him, apparently unaware of Jeff's approach.

"Mr. Ryan said we were not to leave the camp," she said.

"Mr. Ryan," Terpko sneered. "He don't own the world."

"He's in charge of these wagons," Toni said. "I intend to follow his orders."

"Well, I don't!" Terpko said.

"I noticed that," Jeff said, reaching Terpko's side and stopping. "You were told to stick to your driving."

Terpko got up so fast he spilled the food off his plate. "I do my job," he roared. "What I do on my time is my business."

"Not in this train," Jeff said, fighting to control his temper. "Till we get to Colorado, you're under my orders."

"We'll see about that," Terpko said. "You can't stand a little competition with Toni, can you?"

A red mist swam across Jeff's vision. He hadn't even admitted to himself that it was jealousy that was pushing him but Terpko was dragging it out into the open. Jeff knew it was useless to deny it.

He started forward and Terpko lunged at him, swinging a heavy fist. Jeff ducked enough to let most of the forces graze past his ear. He swung with all his might but Terpko twisted so that the blow hit him on the shoulder.

The girls screamed and scrambled out of the way. Bessie moved up closer where she wouldn't miss a blow. Terpko was about the same height as Jeff but twenty pounds heavier. He was no stranger to a brawling fight, Jeff realized before they had exchanged a half dozen blows.

Jeff had been in more fights than he cared to remember but now he dug back into his memory to recall the tricks that had been used on him. Terpko likely knew them all and he wouldn't hesitate to use them.

Jeff caught a sharp blow on the side of his head that made his ears ring. But he didn't back off. He threw two hard punches and had the satisfaction of feeling his fists connect solidly with Terpko's face. A trickle of blood showed at the corner of the latter's mouth.

Jeff gave ground when Terpko charged, taking away the force of his fists. When Terpko slowed, Jeff reversed his direction and put on a charge of his own, raining blows into Terpko's body until he lowered his guard for protection. Jeff quickly raised his aim. His fist smashed Terpko's mouth and nose and blood spurted, giving Jeff the same feeling he'd get if he stepped on a bug.

Terpko went into full retreat then and Jeff kept after

him. Then suddenly he stopped when Terpko produced a short skinning knife from some hidden sheath. Then it was Terpko who advanced, moving in for the kill and Jeff didn't doubt that murder was on his mind.

Beany moved up as though to help but Jeff shook his head, keeping an eye on Terpko's knife hand. Terpko made a couple of unsuccessful lunges, slashing with the knife. Jeff dodged back from the blade each time.

Then, as he circled, he bumped into Beany leaning on a neckyoke he'd taken from a wagon. Jeff remembered Beany's advice. It had sounded ridiculous then; it didn't now. Whipping his arm back, he caught the neckyoke and brought it around in front of him. Terpko's eyes widened as he saw his advantage fade. Still he advanced, knowing that Jeff couldn't swing the neckyoke as fast as he could the knife.

Jeff didn't waste any energy swinging the neckyoke. Terpko could easily dodge it and it would leave Jeff wide open to an attack with the knife. That could be fatal.

Then Terpko feinted one way and drove in from the other. Jeff, anticipating the move, swung the neckyoke at last. He missed Terpko's body but he hit the arm that held the knife. Terpko screamed and jerked himself backward as the knife spun away toward the fire. Jeff leaped over and slapped a foot down on the knife. Holding the neckyoke like a bat, he turned on Terpko.

"Had enough?" he demanded.

Terpko smeared the blood over his face with a hand, growled something, and turned away. Jeff let the neckyoke sag to the ground.

"I'm disgusted," Jeff heard Toni say. "They acted like they were fighting over me."

"They were, honey," Bessie said. "Boy, what would I give to have two young bucks like that fighting over me!"

"Finish your supper," Jeff ordered. "Then get to bed. Zorn, you and I have the first guard tonight."

Jeff came back to the wagon when Beany and Norrie took the middle watch. He wondered if he'd have to watch Terpko closer than the surrounding area while the two took the last watch. But Terpko stayed at his post during that time and ignored Jeff.

It was just at dawn that they came. Jeff saw them first as they sneaked up over the bank of Big Creek to the north of the station.

"Indians!" he shouted.

These were real Indians, he knew, and they were here for scalps and women.

VIII

"Fight from the wagons," Jeff yelled as Beany and Norrie and Zorn rolled out of their blankets.

At Jeff's first shout, a hideous howl came from the Indians who had apparently hoped to get much closer before they were discovered. Jeff dived in behind the wheels of the lead wagon and he saw Terpko do the same at the rear wagon. The other men were under the middle wagon. Beany crawled on his knees and elbows over to the wagon where Jeff had stationed himself.

"Bessie made the girls take their rifles to bed with them in the wagon," Beany said. "Those redskins are going to get a surprise when they open up on them."

"We've got to keep those Indians away from the wagons," Jeff said.

Beany nodded. "How many do you figure there are?"

"Can't get a count yet. Too dark."

"They ain't exactly standing up and waving a flag to let you know where they are, either."

Jeff was surprised at the lack of targets out there in the growing light. He had expected a concentrated rush to try to overpower the camp before it was ready to defend itself.

"Maybe it's just the ones that Bessie fed the other night," he suggested.

"Want another bowl of stew?" Beany yelled.

That brought the first response from the Indians other than that first yell of disappointment. Rifles roared along the creek bank. Jeff and the others answered quickly. A half dozen rifles opened up from the girls' wagon.

"That about answers your question," Jeff said. "If there had been enough of them to overrun us, they'd have charged in immediately. There may be just those five that Bessie fed."

"They'll try to sneak in and pick us off, then steal the girls," Beany predicted.

"Likely," Jeff agreed.

As the light grew stronger, the Indians fired more frequently from the creek bank. The grass around the area had grown high. The station had been abandoned when the railroad reached Fort Hays, about ten miles up Big Creek, three years ago. Jeff would have felt safer if there had been heavy travel on the trail this summer.

Every shot that came from the river was answered by the men and the girls at the wagons. Jeff watched Zorn and Terpko. Terpko was not firing as nonchalantly as he had in the attack the other morning. These were real Indians and they were here to kill. Terpko wasn't ready to die. Jeff still suspected that he had been in cahoots with those other raiders.

A couple of Indians did slip up from the river bank and try to wiggle forward toward the wagons but Jeff spotted one and sent him scurrying back while Terpko nicked the other and discouraged his efforts. Within half an hour the Indians were gone.

"They don't like hot lead any better than calomel," Bessie said as she climbed out of the wagon and began building a fire for breakfast.

Jeff hurried preparations to move out. They wouldn't lose much time because of the raid. During breakfast, he saw Vinton Zorn sitting beside Cheery, telling her some stories that she apparently thought were funny. Jeff didn't like it but he didn't feel the anger that had surged through him when Terpko had tried to monopolize Toni's time.

As they were hitching up the teams, Zorn strolled past Jeff. "Are you going to try to lay me out with a neckyoke, too?" he asked softly.

Jeff stared at the gambler, realizing that he had been talking to Cheery partly to throw down a challenge to Jeff. "According to how far out of line you get," he said.

"Are you as good at swinging a gun as you are a neckyoke?" Zorn asked, the challenge clear in his voice.

"Afraid to try it with fists?" Jeff asked.

Zorn scowled. "I don't fight with fists. That's for crude numbskulls."

"Killing a man with a gun isn't crude, I suppose?"

Jeff turned away in disgust. Zorn apparently lived by his cards and survived by his gun. Jeff had no special talent with a gun but he could use it if he had to. He probably wouldn't have much chance against someone with the confidence and skill of Zorn but he'd make sure he was never without his gun as long as Zorn was with the train.

Jeff wondered how interested Zorn was in Cheery. He was a good friend of Hod Terpko's. He might just be testing Jeff on behalf of Terpko, trying to get him into a gun battle. It wouldn't happen, Jeff resolved.

Zorn went out of his way to be with Cheery at every opportunity, especially during the meals. They had just passed the old Lookout Station on the B. O. D. when they stopped for dinner. The wagons were not loaded heavily and they were making good progress.

They passed Louise Springs during the afternoon. There was little sign of the station that had been established there when the trail was laid out. It had been abandoned in favor of Storm Hollow, above five miles farther west. Jeff had that station as his goal for the night. It was actually early camping time when they reached it.

After Bessie and Star had supper ready, Zorn sought

out Cheery and sat down beside her while he ate. Beany, sitting close to Jeff, pointed a fork at them.

"Are you going to have to dehorn that jasper, too?" he muttered.

"He'd like to have me try—with guns."

Beany shook his head. "I wouldn't cross guns with him."

"Don't figure to."

Before the meal was over, Terpko came by, having emptied his plate. "How about Zorn?" he asked Jeff. "Going to let him run with the fillies?"

"He wasn't hired to drive a team," Jeff said. "So he's not my responsibility."

"Afraid of him, ain't you?" Terpko grunted and moved on.

"You may have to cut that little tinhorn down to size," Beany said. "Just make sure he can't get to a gun when you jump him."

"We've had enough trouble," Jeff said.

He frowned as he turned his attention again to Zorn and Cheery. Cheery seemed to be enjoying Zorn's company. Maybe it was because she hadn't had too much attention on this trip and, pretty as she was, she likely was used to plenty of it.

Maybe he was afraid of Zorn, Jeff thought. He wasn't a gun fighter. If it came to a showdown, Jeff knew he would face the gambler. But fighting with a tinhorn gambler would gain him nothing, even if he won.

When Zorn tired of talking to Cheery, he climbed up on the seat of one of the wagons with a handful of little rocks and began pelting Hercules with them. It took the goat only a few seconds to locate his tormentor. He bleated angrily and sized up the wagon. Jeff thought for a moment that he was going to try to jump into the wagon where Zorn was. Zorn apparently thought the same because he stopped throwing the rocks and waited until the goat was called away from the wagon by Star. Jeff had heard that a goat didn't give up a victim easily once he had him cornered.

"What do you think you gained by teasing that goat?" Beany asked Zorn when he got down.

"I'll shoot him next time," Zorn snapped angrily.

"Maybe you'd better," Beany said. "I hear that goats have memories like elephants. He may tree you again and keep you there," he snickered. "You sure did look cute, though, perched up there like a scared bird, afraid to move."

"I wasn't afraid," Zorn shot back.

"It must be wonderful to be as bra-a-a-ave as you are," Beany bleated, closely imitating Hercules.

Zorn seemed torn between running and drawing his gun. He finally whirled and headed out to picket the horse he'd been assigned to ride. Beany snickered again.

Jeff turned to the wagon where the girls were congregated. "Glad you called off your goat," he said to Star.

"I was afraid he'd shoot him or I'd have let Hercules keep him up there all night," Star said.

"He wasn't really hurting Hercules," Cheery put in. "Vinton just has a playful nature."

Jeff frowned. He wondered if Cheery really was fooled so completely by the gambler. He looked at Toni but she turned her eyes away. She evidently hadn't forgiven him for getting into that fight with Terpko. He turned away and Bessie caught up with him.

"There's something about that little gambler that stinks," she said. "I don't like him any better than that goat does."

"He rubs me wrong, too," Jeff said. "I'm keeping an eye on him."

"A gun would be more effective than your eye," Bessie muttered.

Jeff half expected Zorn to stir up more trouble. He'd been treed by the goat and Beany had rubbed his fur the wrong way. But the gambler was evidently satisfied to let things quiet down.

Jeff got the wagons off to a good start the next morning and stopped for noon close to the old White Rock Station. He was determined to reach Downer Station for the night camp. He cut the noon stop a little short and actually reached Downer Creek with the sun still a ways up in the sky.

While camp was being set up, Jeff rode to the top of a hill nearby and surveyed the surrounding country. They were far enough west and south of Fort Hays now that Indians would not be afraid to attack a small wagon train. The attack on them a few mornings ago had convinced Jeff that the stories he'd heard about peace on the plains were premature.

Below him, he saw three of the girls leave the camp

and go to the nearby creek for water. He recognized Lily by her height and he guessed one of the other two was Star because Hercules was trailing the three to the creek.

As he watched, they reached the creek but before they could dip up any water, two Indians suddenly charged out of the tall grass close to the creek. Jeff could hear the girls scream all the way up to the hill where he sat on his horse.

Jeff spurred his horse toward the creek but it seemed the animal was moving in slow motion. Down below, he saw the entire drama unfold.

Each Indian grabbed one of the smaller girls. Jeff had guessed that the third girl was Cheery. Although no Indian had her, Lily joined the other two in screaming loud enough to raise the dead.

The Indians apparently were too engrossed in what they were doing to see what was going on just around them. As Star continued to scream, Hercules responded to her cries for help. She had said he was her guardian: now he proved it.

Jeff saw him rear up on his back legs. That expression of anger usually ended in a charge. This time was no exception.

The Indian trying to drag Star toward the two ponies hidden behind the creek bank fifty yards downstream either failed to notice or ignored the goat. He must surely have wished a moment later that he were facing a gun rather than the woolly tornado that struck him. Hercules had enough experience to know that a hard boost from the rear usually upended his two-legged enemies. He gave this red-skinned foe a terrific boost because the Indian was taken completely by surprise.

The Indian went over like a broken reed in a hurricane. Star had the misfortune to be clutched tightly to the Indian and he landed right on top of her. But he kept rolling and his grip was broken. Star was on her feet before the Indian was. In fact, the Indian didn't quite make it. He was on his hands and knees, shaking his head in dazed bewilderment, when Hercules caught up with him again. This time the Indian was propelled like a cannon ball over the bank where he splashed unceremoniously into the creek.

Jeff was also watching the Indian who had grabbed Cheery. At the commotion created by the goat's charge, that Indian had stopped momentarily and stared at his companion. It was at that exact second that Lily took a hand in the activities. She stopped screaming and leaped at Cheery's captor. She was half a head taller than the brave and her fury matched the Indian's determination to make off with his prize.

Lily caught an arm of the Indian and jerked him away from Cheery like a dog tearing a bone away from a cat. Cheery went spinning but never lost her feet. The Indian wheeled toward this new menace just in time for Lily to grab him around the waist. As he struggled, her hand dropped to his leg and she lifted him like a sack of meal above her head. With one whirl, she let him go. Jeff could almost feel the jarring of the ground when he hit.

He started to get up when he saw Lily coming after him. But Lily was cheated out of her fun by Hercules.

His first target having disappeared over the bank into the river, the goat turned on this new enemy who had been plunked down on the ground not far from him.

That Indian had just risen enough to make a perfect target for Hercules. The Indian threw up his hands as if to ward off this apparition from another world when Hercules made contact. The Indian flew over the bank with all the velocity of his partner and he splashed into the creek with a mighty grunt.

With no targets left, Hercules ran to the bank and glared over at the Indians. If they had not been in the water, Jeff was sure he would have pursued them farther. But water was something Hercules didn't relish. He shook his beard angrily and Jeff was close enough now to hear his bleat. The Indians sent water in all directions as they scrambled away, trying to run before they got completely to their feet, threatening to splash all the water out of the creek in their haste. By the time Jeff arrived at the creek bank, the Indians had disappeared up the creek toward their horses.

"Anybody hurt?" Jeff demanded of the girls.

"Pride's all," Lily said. "I wanted one more whack at that dirty varmint."

"I think he had enough," Jeff said and reined his horse upstream. It was then that he heard the galloping hoofs of the Indians' ponies. The camp would see no more of those two, he was positive. Lily and Hercules had made sure of that.

Jeff turned back just as Zorn came running down from the wagons. He went straight to Cheery.

"What happened? I got here as fast as I could."

"Indians," Cheery said breathlessly. "One of them grabbed me. Lily ran him off."

"I wish I could have gotten here quicker," Zorn said. "I'd have killed the filthy snake for touching such a fragile beauty as you."

Cheery's fear-strained face softened. "I know you would," she said gently.

"You'll never be in danger when I'm around," Zorn said.

All the others from the wagons had arrived now. Bessie snorted when she heard Zorn. "She's in danger whenever *you* are around," she snapped.

Norrie, who usually kept quiet around the other men, now pushed up to Zorn. "Bessie's right," he said in a voice shrill with anger and fear. "You're a bigger danger than any Indian."

"Why, you little punk!" Zorn snapped, whirling around like a bee-stung dog. "I'll teach you to have some respect."

Before Norrie had a chance to duck, Zorn swung a fist that caught Norrie on the side of the head. He spun around and dropped like a clubbed calf. Jeff was there then and he left his saddle in a leap, landing in front of Zorn as he was reaching for Norrie to hit him again. He caught the gambler by the shirt front and jerked him back.

"Pick on someone your size," Jeff said sharply.

"I'll whip anybody who says what he said to me," Zorn said.

"Consider it said again," Jeff retorted. "By me."

Zorn glared at Jeff but made no attempt to hit him.

"I'm unarmed. Why don't you say that when I've got a gun?" he said, breathing hard.

"Norrie didn't have a gun. I won't need mine."

Zorn glared at Jeff, hatred in his eyes. But he jerked away and started back toward the wagons. Jeff knew the time could not be far away when he would face a showdown with Zorn.

IX

Jeff pulled his gaze away from Zorn's back and turned to the girls who had tangled with the Indians. Star was on her knees, hugging her goat. For once, Jeff had to agree that the goat deserved some reward for his performance. If those Indians believed in a place of punishment in the hereafter, they must have thought that Hercules was a harbinger of that place.

Lily was describing all the action to Bessie and Beany and the two girls who had not been at the river, Posey and Toni. Terpko was standing off by himself as if it was beneath his dignity to show concern.

It was Cheery, though, that Jeff wanted to talk to. He found her beside Norrie who was sitting up, rubbing his head. Jeff crossed to them.

"You all right, Norrie?" he asked.

"I reckon," Norrie said. "He hit me before I knew he was going to fight."

"A man like Vinton Zorn always strikes without warning," Jeff said. "Like a sidewinder. It gives him an advantage."

"Norrie shouldn't have said what he did," Cheery said. "But Vinton had no call to hit Norrie."

"I'm glad you see that, at least," Jeff said. "He's no good, especially for you."

Cheery rubbed a hand gently over the bruise on Norrie's jaw. "That is going to be sore," she said.

"It already is," Norrie said. "But he was bragging how he'd protect you and he won't. He didn't this afternoon, anyway."

Cheery didn't seem to hear what he said. "He shouldn't have hit you," she repeated and went to join the other girls.

"You'd better stay away from Zorn for a while till he cools down," Jeff suggested to Norrie.

"Reckon I will," Norrie said, "unless he starts mooning over Cheery again. I can't stand that."

Jeff grinned. "You might stop that quicker by talking to Cheery."

Norrie's face turned red. "I ain't going to tell her what to do."

"You're not liable to tell Zorn, either," Jeff said. "Unless you do better than you just did. Let's get back to camp before those Indians come back and steal our supper."

Norrie scrambled to his feet and headed back to his chore of staking out the horses close to the wagons to graze through the night. Most of the others had already returned to the camp or were going. Cheery fell in step with Jeff.

"Vinton shouldn't have hit Norrie," she repeated. "Why did he back off when you stood up to him?"

"I'm bigger than Norrie," Jeff said.

"I didn't think he'd back off from you," Cheery said. "Maybe I shouldn't tell you this but he said he was going to take over the wagon train."

Jeff shot a glance at Cheery. She was serious. "How does he figure on doing that?"

"By driving you away, I suppose," Cheery said. "He said he could get the train through and you couldn't."

"I wonder why he thinks I can't get it through," Jeff said, his mind flashing toward possible reasons for Zorn's statement.

"I don't know. He said once that you wouldn't live to get to Colorado."

Jeff nodded. "That sounds more like the tinhorn I figure he is. He probably plans on gunning me down."

"He wouldn't do that," Cheery said quickly, then added softly, "would he?"

"Not if I can help it," Jeff said. "Thanks for telling me, Cheery."

Jeff turned toward Beany when he reached the first wagon. On his way, he passed on the other side of a wagon from Zorn and Terpko. Jeff had not been without his gun any waking minute since he had become convinced that Zorn intended to force him into a gun fight if he could. It was probably lucky for him that the girls' screams had brought Zorn running from camp at a moment when he had not had his gun strapped on.

Jeff paused when he heard Zorn talking angrily to Terpko on the other side of the wagon.

"He's butted into my affairs once too often."

"I wouldn't advise tackling him with your fists," Terpko said. "You ain't big enough."

"I'm not a fist fighter," Zorn said condescendingly. "My gun will do my fighting for me. He's got no right to butt in on Cheery and me."

"You don't want her," Terpko said. "She's only a kid."

"She likes me. And if I want her, I'll get her, too, any time I please."

Jeff listened intently. If Zorn had ideas of getting Cheery without her consent, he wanted to know it.

"How do you figure on doing that?" Terpko asked, more amused than curious.

"I know where she sleeps," Zorn said. "I can snatch her out of her blankets and the other girls won't even miss her till morning."

The two stopped talking and Jeff moved quietly on. That was a ridiculous idea Zorn had. But he just might try it. Zorn did not always act like a rational man. Even his method of getting into the wagon train was on the bizarre side, claiming he was lost and had escaped from Indians.

Jeff turned toward Bessie starting supper. Bessie saw him coming and frowned.

"Supper won't be ready for another half hour," she said gruffly.

"I can wait," Jeff said. "There's something else that maybe can't."

Bessie stopped slicing off the chunk of meat for the supper stew and stared at Jeff. "Something about the girls?"

"One of them," Jeff said. "Cheery."

"Then that tinhorn is involved, ain't he?"

Jeff nodded. "I just heard him talking to Terpko on the other side of the wagon. He said he might grab Cheery some night. He knows where she sleeps."

"Oh, he does?" Bessie said indignantly. "He must have been snooping around."

"Does Cheery sleep in the same place every night?"

Bessie nodded. "She don't like to be crowded. If we're in the wagon, there's no way to avoid it. But if it's warm like it will be tonight, she sleeps well out away from the other girls."

"Maybe you'd better sleep closer to her," Jeff suggested.

"I've got a better idea," Bessie said and went back to slicing the meat.

"Make sure it's a good one. I'd hate to see Zorn kidnap Cheery. I think she's beginning to see through him. She didn't like the way he hit Norrie."

"If she had any eyes at all, she'd see that Norrie is moon-eyed over her."

Supper was late because of the interruption caused by the Indians. It was almost dark when Bessie called them to eat. Jeff shot a look at Zorn occasionally and caught him twice studying Jeff with a steady gaze. Zorn looked away quickly each time. Once he found Zorn staring at Cheery. He wasn't trying to sit with her tonight.

He should kick Zorn out of camp. The gambler hadn't been invited to travel with them. They had treated him like any rescued prairie victim and fed him. That was the extent of their responsibility. But

Jeff knew that if he drove him away without a good reason, the others would think it was because he was afraid of the gambler, whether they said as much or not.

After checking the horses to make sure all picket pins were secure, Jeff came back to his blankets. Beany and Terpko had the first watch tonight. Beany was standing watch to the west while Terpko took his post to the east where the horses were picketed.

Jeff moved his blankets nearer the lead wagon where he could keep an eye on Zorn. Zorn was already in bed. He would have the last watch tonight with Beany while Jeff and Norrie took the middle watch.

Jeff had trouble staying awake but he wanted to keep an eye on Zorn. The gambler was not one to put off anything once he had decided to do it. He crowded Jeff closer to a gun battle at every opportunity. If he had really decided to kidnap Cheery, he would likely do it tonight.

Jeff was almost asleep when Zorn slipped quietly out of his blankets. He came fully awake but he didn't move. Zorn looked in all directions before gliding toward the rear of the wagons, bypassing the center wagon where the girls were sleeping.

Picking up his saddle and blanket, he moved out toward the horses. Jeff got up and followed quietly. It wasn't very dark with a clear sky, lots of stars and half a moon. Still he had to get closer to see what Zorn was doing.

Zorn saddled his horse. Terpko was close by but he didn't say anything. Apparently they had reached an understanding on this before supper. At first, Jeff thought hopefully that Zorn was riding out of camp. But when he got his horse saddled, he turned back toward the wagons.

Jeff retreated to his blankets, in case Zorn checked, and wanted to see what he would do next. Straight as an arrow, he went toward the girl sleeping a short distance from the others. Moving silently, he reached the sleeping form, then swiftly his hand darted down and covered the mouth of the sleeper while his other arm scooped her up.

Jeff started out of his blankets, then stopped. Zorn hadn't lifted the girl the way he apparently had thought he could. Then Jeff saw why. It wasn't Cheery that Zorn had grabbed. It was Bessie. She had traded places with Cheery.

Bessie struggled to her feet before Zorn fully realized his mistake. She jerked free from the gambler and swung a fist like a man. Zorn ducked but then Bessie caught him by the hair with one hand while she whaled him with her other fist.

Zorn forgot his attempt to be quiet and began yelling as if Indians were scalping him. Jeff doubted if scalping would be any more painful than the way Bessie was hanging onto his hair with one hand and trying to knock his head loose from it with the other.

Bessie in her nightgown looked as big as the side of a barn and likely she looked even bigger to Zorn. He tried to fight back but the pain of having his hair pulled with such force weakened his blows and made him howl like a banshee.

Jeff made no attempt to interfere. No licking he could give Zorn would be as painful or as humiliating as what he was now getting. The girls were all awake and all but Cheery were yelling encouragement to Bessie. Jeff didn't think that she really needed any. She seemed to be enjoying herself immensely.

Hercules, attracted by the commotion, loped around the wagons and stared at the whirling nightgown and Zorn's flying heels. He chose the nightgown and charged. Bessie saw him coming, however, and wheeled Zorn around just in time to take the full force of the charging goat's head. Zorn's yell rose to a shriek as he was rocketed forward.

Star came running and caught the goat and pulled him back. Bessie, hands on hips, stared at Zorn while the gambler, on hands and knees, looked up at her like a whipped dog.

"That time, gambler man, you didn't play your cards right," Bessie snapped.

"That was a stacked deck if I ever saw one," Beany said.

"Zorn," Jeff said, moving up to face the gambler, "you've already got your horse saddled. Ride."

"That's our horse," Beany howled. "Make him walk."

"He can get farther away if he rides," Jeff said. "I want him as far from this camp by sun-up as he can get."

Zorn, holding one hand on his head as if to keep his hair on, was in no condition to argue. He turned and moved slowly toward the horses.

"Old Herc can help you if can't hurry any faster," Beany yelled after him.

Zorn managed a faster pace, disappearing among the horses. A minute later, Jeff saw his silhouette as he swung up on his horse and rode to the north.

"He won't go far," Beany predicted to Jeff.

"At least he's out of the way for the moment."

Jeff doubted if Zorn would leave the country until Jeff himself had beaten him. He could never survive the humiliation of having a woman beat him up until he had to leave camp. He'd come back, gun at the ready, looking for Jeff.

Jeff tried to sleep but he couldn't. He found that he wasn't alone. He saw one of the girls leave her bed and come toward him, wrapped in a blanket. He sat up in his blankets when he recognized Cheery.

"I couldn't sleep," Cheery said as she knelt on the ground close to Jeff. "Vinton disappointed me. He really did intend to kidnap me. I didn't believe it when Bessie told me but I traded places with her, anyway. You have to do what Bessie says."

Jeff grinned. "Even Zorn found that out."

"I thought I should tell you something he told me. He talked a lot, you know. He told me there was a man in Colorado that we'd see one of these days who would help him beat you if he couldn't do it alone. His name was Grillo or Grilli or something like that."

Jeff jerked upright as if an electric shock had jolted him. "Ross Grilli?"

Cheery nodded. "That's the name. Do you know him?"

"I've been looking for him," Jeff said. "Did Zorn say where he was?"

Cheery shook her head. "Only that he was in Colorado. I thought you ought to know that."

"Thanks for telling me, Cheery," Jeff said. "I do need to know it."

Cheery went back to her bedroll, leaving Jeff wider awake than ever. How did Grilli know that Jeff was coming west? He obviously did or Zorn wouldn't have expected Grilli to help him get rid of Jeff. Did Grilli know somehow that Beany had gone to Kansas City after Jeff?

Ten minutes before it was time for Jeff and Norrie to relieve Beany and Terpko on guard duty, Jeff got out of his blankets and went out to the place where Beany was standing guard.

"Cheery just told me Zorn said that Grilli would show up to help him do away with me." Jeff said softly. "Are you sure you don't know Grilli? Somehow he has found out I'm coming to Colorado."

"I don't know anybody named Grilli," Beany said. "What does he look like? He may be using a different handle."

"He's about thirty. Not quite six feet tall and weighs about two hundred pounds. Has black hair and eyes."

"Gossy!" Beany exclaimed. "That describes Abe's new hand to a T."

Jeff nodded. "Sure. Ross Grilli-Gossy. He said he'd get even with me. He never knows when he *is* even. He likely figures to hit at Uncle Abe to get at me. I've got to get out there before he does something to Uncle Abe."

Beany held up a hand. "Don't push on the reins, Jeff. Abe said for you to bring these girls to his ranch. If you leave your job here, he won't give you any partnership. You know Abe. All you'll get will be a good tongue lashing."

Jeff frowned. "You're right. Uncle Abe wouldn't consider saving his skin an excuse for leaving the job I promised to do. Does Grilli know Uncle Abe is planning to take me in the partner on the AR?"

Beany shook his head. "Couldn't. I'm the only one Abe told. But the hands did know I was to bring you back."

"That might explain the things that have happened to me if Grilli got word to his friends in Kansas City. Like the day before we left when I got beaten up and almost killed. And when I was decoyed into falling over that cliff. Terpko or Zorn could have been responsible for both of those."

"Now Zorn is out to get you in a gun fight and kill you. Figures—if this Grilli would go that far to keep you from finding him."

"He's a greedy man and if he has figured a way to steal Uncle Abe blind, he'd do anything to keep me from stopping him."

Beany rubbed his chin worriedly. "We'll push on as fast as we can. But you'd better stay here with the wagon like you promised."

Jeff didn't argue but he was worried about Abe. Grilli might be planning something on Abe's AR ranch that would mean a big loss to Abe, maybe even his life. Otherwise, Grilli surely wouldn't be so intent on keeping Jeff from getting there. Zorn certainly was working with Grilli. Probably Terpko, too. Zorn had been mighty loose tongued with Cheery but maybe he had wanted Cheery to tell Jeff so Jeff would be worried and upset enough to take foolish chances when the showdown came.

Jeff stayed on watch the rest of the night then rode on ahead as the wagons started out. He didn't know what to expect but with his new conclusions about Zorn and Grilli, he had to be prepared for anything.

When he caught a movement off to his right in the hills, he wasn't surprised but he was tense. There was trouble out there and he had to check it out.

X

Jeff reined up his horse and studied his surroundings, trying not to look directly at the place where he had caught the movement. It could be only an antelope or a coyote but he didn't think so.

He saw Beany coming from the wagons on his mule, Angel, with Samson trotting behind. Beany evidently had been watching Jeff and had correctly concluded that something had roused his suspicions.

Jeff started slowly on, reining his horse at right angles to the movement he had seen. He had gone only a short distance when he saw it again. This time he pin-pointed it. He still didn't know what it was. It had flashed above a little knoll quickly and then just as quickly disappeared.

Beany arrived at an awkward trot. Angel refused to be prodded into a run. Beany slowed the mule to keep pace with Jeff's horse.

"What did you see?"

"I don't know," Jeff said. "Was it so obvious that I saw something?"

"It was to me," Beany said. "I was expecting something to happen. Where did you see it?"

"Off to the right behind that knoll. It showed twice, each time for just a second."

"Maybe Indians," Beany suggested.

"Indians are seldom careless enough to let themselves be seen until they are ready," Jeff said. "This is more than likely somebody who wants to be seen."

"Are you going to ignore it?"

"Can't afford to," Jeff said. "We're sure Zorn is hanging around somewhere. And Grilli may be here, too. If we don't keep them busy, they might lay an ambush for the wagons."

"They might catch Toni," Beany said, a twinkle in his eye.

"Aw, shut up," Jeff grunted. "If that is Zorn or Grilli, he may be just waiting till one of us gets in rifle range."

"Likely," Beany agreed. "But it's you they want, not me." Beany let his eyes run over the hills and swales to the north of the trail. "Looks to me like Angel and me could come around from the east and sneak up on his backside while he was watching you. That is, providing you can quiet your curiosity long enough to give Angel time to amble over that way."

"He'll be watching you."

"Not if you keep him occupied. I'll go back to the wagons and cut north behind that hill. He won't see me."

Jeff nodded. "Agreed. But don't get careless. Wouldn't want you or Angel to get hurt. Especially Angel."

"Anybody hurts Angel is going to be sorry." Beany reined the mule around and trotted back toward the wagons which were still half a mile behind Jeff.

Jeff dismounted and pretended to work on his saddle cinch. He didn't want to move far from here. If he did if that was an ambusher, he would move, too, and Beany would lose track of him.

Twice more Jeff saw the flash from the top of the knoll. He was sure it was a hat briefly flipped into the air, not giving Jeff time to really identify it. Jeff ignored it, scanning the prairie to the west and glancing back at the wagons now and then as if he felt he had gotten too far ahead of them and was waiting.

He saw Beany reach the wagons and almost immediately rein off to the north and disappear from Jeff's view to the east of the ridge. He would have been out of sight of whoever or whatever was behind the knoll Jeff was watching.

Jeff waited until he figured that Angel, even at the mule's slow pace, should have reached a point not too far from the spot where Jeff had seen the movement. Then he mounted and reined his horse at an angle to the ridge and moved ahead at a walk. He was gradually getting closer to the spot he had pinpointed. If there was a man there trying to get a shot at him, he'd be waiting to squeeze the trigger and likely wouldn't look for an enemy behind him.

Suddenly the rifle roared and Jeff flinched although the shot fell far short. The man may have gotten too anxious and his long wait had warped his sense of distance.

Jeff jerked his rifle from the boot. The ambusher was out of range but he might come charging over the hill to get a better shot. Jeff intended to be ready.

He wasn't ready for what he saw, however. There was an explosion of action right at the crest of the knoll. Jeff recognized Vinton Zorn as he suddenly leaped up and dropped the rifle. A dog was tearing at the leg of his pants. Jeff guessed instantly what had happened. Samson had some hunting blood in him and apparently Beany had sent him after Zorn and the dog had sneaked up on Zorn before the gambler knew he was near. Now Samson, urged on by Beany, was chewing on Zorn's leg.

Zorn was yelling like a wounded hyena, kicking furiously at the dog, and running toward his horse which evidently was just behind the knoll. Jeff kicked his horse into a run toward the action. Since Zorn had dropped his rifle at the first surprise attack from Samson, Jeff wasn't worried about a gun battle now.

Reaching the crest of the knoll, Jeff saw Zorn on his horse racing off to the northeast with Samson giving chase, nipping at the horse's heels. The horse kicked wildly each time he was nipped, almost unseating Zorn.

Jeff urged his horse into a hard gallop after the

fleeing gambler but he soon reined up. Samson had excited Zorn's horse until he was running all out now, even keeping away from the dog. There was no way that Jeff could catch him. He looked around for Beany. Beany and Angel were coming at that same lumbering trot, Angel's best speed unless urged on by something more determined than Beany's spurless heels.

"Guess Samson flushed him out in the open, didn't he?" Beany said, his face split with a wide grin.

"Zorn may not get that horse stopped till he hits Big Creek," Jeff agreed.

"Too bad we didn't get close enough to stop his clock."

"So far, he's been humiliated by Bessie and chased by a dog. His gunman's pride will make him try again just to save face. He might decide to circle back to the wagon now."

"He'll have to slow that horse down before he can circle anywhere," Beany said. "Here comes Samson. He figures he'd done his day's work."

"He has," Jeff said. "If Zorn hadn't gotten too anxious, he might have had a better shot at me. I was still too far away."

Beany nodded. "Yeah. But Samson wasn't. That was Zorn's only shot even if he didn't know it then. I'm going to ride over and pick up his rifle."

Jeff turned to scan the horizon to the west. He had the feeling that there was more danger off to the northeast where Zorn had disappeared than there was ahead of them. But his job was to make sure the wagons didn't run into trouble.

By the time Beany had collected the rifle, Jeff had decided to go back to the wagons to make sure Zorn had not circled back there. Then he'd return to his place ahead of the train.

The wagons had stopped when Jeff and Beany came back over the knoll in sight of the train. Jeff didn't like that. He turned to Beany.

"Did you tell them to stop?"

Beany shook his head. "We'd better get down there in a hurry."

Zorn kept running through Jeff's mind. The wagons were east of Jeff and Beany. Zorn could have turned his horse down to them once the dog stopped chasing him. If he was there, he'd likely demand a showdown with Jeff. That had been his goal since he first joined the train; likely had been the reason he had waylaid the wagons. Grilli had probably given him those orders. He might not even be a gambler as he claimed but there was no doubt in Jeff's mind that he was a gunman.

There was no way to be cautious in their approach to the wagons. They were out in the open and so were the wagons. If Zorn was there, they'd have to ride right in on him. Jeff saw Bessie, Norrie and Terpko with several of the girls near the second wagon.

Swinging off his horse as he reached the first wagon, Jeff looked for a reason why the wagons had stopped. Then his suspicions were confirmed. Vinton Zorn stepped around the corner of the middle wagon, holding Toni in front of him.

"Looking for me?" Zorn asked.

Jeff's hand pulled away from his gun. Zorn didn't have his gun in his hand but he had Toni. She was more protection for him than his gun.

"I was hoping I'd seen the last of you," Jeff said.

"I'll bet you were," Zorn said. "I'll let this little lady go when you step out where we can have a fair fight."

"Don't do it," Toni said quickly. "He wants to kill you."

The warning wasn't necessary but Toni had risked retaliation from Zorn in giving it.

"He's wanted to kill me for a long time," he said. "Maybe he deserves a chance to try."

Jeff saw Beany dismount from his mule near the head wagon and disappear behind it. Star had moved back from the group near the middle wagon and now she was beckoning to Hercules at the rear of the last wagon. Interruptions were coming but they weren't likely to arrive in time to prevent a killing.

"No gun fighting allowed in camp!" Bessie yelled shrilly.

Zorn laughed. "If this is a camp, then you'd better move it quick. There's going to be some powder burned here."

He suddenly pushed Toni to one side but she jumped back at him. He shoved her roughly away again, never taking his eyes from Jeff. Jeff returned his stare.

Then Jeff saw that Hercules had recognized Zorn, the enemy who had tormented him so much. Zorn wasn't aware of the goat's presence until he heard his angry bleat. Wheeling around, he saw Hercules on his hind legs, his head shaking, the preliminary to his charge.

Zorn reached for his gun but at that instant Samson charged at him from another angle. Jeff saw Beany behind the wagon, urging the dog on. Samson hadn't forgotten the target he'd had out there on the prairie and here it was again, waiting for him.

Zorn wheeled on around when he heard Samson's growl. Jeff ran toward the gunman who had his back to him now, knowing that he might wheel and fire at him any second. But the dog grabbed his leg and the goat was only yards away, charging fast. Zorn forgot about his battle with Jeff. He leaped for the wagon, landing on the hub of the rear wheel. From there he climbed to the top of the big wheel, holding with one hand to the bow that supported the canvas top.

Zorn clawed his gun free and swung it around. But Jeff was there then and he jerked Zorn's foot off the slippery iron tire of the wheel and he came down with a crash, his gun flying almost to the front of the wagon.

Beany called Samson back and Star caught Hercules before he could do more than butt Zorn once. Jeff jerked the gambler to his feet. Zorn came up fighting. Jeff relished the prospect of a hand to hand fight.

The fight didn't last long, however; Jeff released his fury in two vicious blows to Zorn's head and Zorn reeled back against the wagon wheel and slowly slid down to a sitting position on the ground.

"You'd better finish him," Beany said.

Jeff knew what he meant. But Zorn was unarmed now. It would be murder to shoot him. He jerked Zorn to his feet again.

"I'll give you just two minutes to get out of range of

this gun. One second longer and I start shooting."

"My gun?" Zorn mumbled.

"Leave it where it it. Think about your hide."

Zorn took Jeff at his word. He sprinted for his horse and was almost out of sight when the two minutes were up.

"Should have beefed him," Beany said. "He's like a rattler. If you don't cut his head off, he'll still bite you."

"He may have had enough this time," Jeff said hopefully. "Let's get the wagons moving. Every minute we lose gives Grilli that much more time for his mischief."

Jeff didn't relax his vigil, however, as the wagons moved on the next day. When they reached Fort Wallace in western Kansas, everyone was ready for a rest. But Jeff gave them only the remainder of the day off.

Jeff rode over to the fort sitting on the slope to the north of Pond Creek and talked to the officers he found there, asking about Vinton Zorn and Ross Grilli. One lieutenant said that a man answering Zorn's description had been there but no one resembling Grilli.

Jeff got back to camp in time for supper. Beany met him. "Terpko has been gone all afternoon," he reported. "Said there was nothing to do here so he went for a ride. That don't make sense. After being on the trail all the way across Kansas, he gets half a day to rest and he goes for a ride."

Jeff nodded. "We'd better make him tell us where he went and who he saw."

"You figure the way to do it and I'll help."

Jeff went on to the fire where Bessie was getting supper. Terpko was also checking on supper.

Bessie suddenly wheeled on Terpko. "Get off that line!" she yelled.

Terpko jumped back as if he'd been stung. "What line?"

"That one you was standing on," she roared. "I drew that to keep bad luck away. All day everything has been pointing to bad luck. Lily got her dress on backward. Samson has been chasing his tail. Now I try to put the jinx on the bad luck and you blunder up and break the spell."

Terpko backed away another step. "I don't know nothing about your spells," he grumbled. "You and your superstitions!"

"Go ahead and make fun of the signs," Bessie bellowed. "That will bring you more bad luck."

Terpko retreated hastily. Jeff grinned. Terpko was afraid of Bessie's superstitions. It suddenly gave him an idea. He approached Bessie, careful to step over the line without touching it.

"How about some help, Bessie?" he asked. "Terpko knows something we've got to find out. If you'll help us scare him with your superstitions, he might talk."

Bessie scowled at Jeff. "You lame brain!" she snapped. "You think my premonitions are superstitions, don't you? I can read signs. If they point bad, then we're in for bad luck. I don't mess around with those signs."

Jeff shrugged. Bessie wouldn't help unless her signs were right. But the idea still lingered in the back of his

113

mind. If Terpko could be convinced that his luck was going bad, he might be scared into telling some of his secrets.

At daylight, Jeff led the wagons away from Fort Wallace. Crossing the railroad tracks a short distance west of the fort and the little town, he followed the old Butterfield Overland Despatch trail. He hoped to get to the Colorado line before camping tonight.

Beany was with Jeff in the afternoon when they came to the stand of big cottonwoods that had been a landmark on the trail. Many had been cut down for firewood and to make repairs on wagons. But there was still a big grove of them. Big Timbers Station on the B. O. D. had been here. It would make a good place to camp for the night.

Suddenly Beany jerked back on the reins of Angel. "Listen," he whispered.

Jeff listened and heard the soft moan that rose almost to a shriek then subsided again to a moan. It was coming from the big trees. In spite of himself, Jeff felt a chill travel along the spine as the eerie moan swelled again.

XI

"Is th-th-that a ghost?" Beany whispered.

"Don't tell me you believe in ghosts," Jeff chided. But he felt a sudden urge to put distance between himself and that sound. Yet he had to know what was causing it.

"I know that these big trees were a favorite campground for Indians even before the white men found them," Beany said, pulling back so hard on Angel's reins that the mule began backing.

Jeff nodded. "They were also a burial ground for them." He grinned. "Maybe it is a ghost. Do you suppose we can make Terpko think it is a ghost coming after him?"

"If he hears that sound, he'll believe anything you tell him. That would scare the meanness out of Satan himself."

"Let's find out who or what is doing it," Jeff said.

He knew he was sounding braver than he actually was. That shriek that subsided to a moan then rose to a shriek again was unnerving. Even the horse and mule were alarmed so Jeff dismounted and handed the reins to Beany.

"You keep my horse handy. I may be in a hurry to get out of here when I come back."

"I'm in a hurry right now," Beany said. "I can think of lots of things I ought to be doing somewhere else."

Jeff walked slowly toward the trees. The moan rose

to a shriek again but Jeff couldn't locate the source of the sound. It wasn't on the ground; it seemed to me coming from the branches of the tree.

He saw a few of the old Indian burial platforms in the tree branches but they had been ransacked for any valuables buried with the dead. The white travelers passing here had likely done that. The Indians wrapped their dead in blankets and placed their finest possessions on the platform with them to be taken to the Happy Hunting Ground.

As Jeff got closer, he saw that there were some new burials here. Some old Indians apparently had requested that their bodies be brought back to this burial site, now that the whites had abandoned this trail in favor of the railroad.

Then Jeff pinpointed the source of the moan and shriek. It rose to a crescendo just as he was nearing the latest of the burial platforms. The sound was coming from that platform. He looked around nervously. There was no one in sight. That sound was not made by human throat.

Gingerly, Jeff climbed into the tree to view the dead Indian. It was then that he saw the mouth organ lying beside the corpse. Apparently the old Indian had been given this mouth harp and he had treasured it. When he died, it was placed beside him on the platform. The breeze was blowing through the harp, making a moan when the breeze was light, rising to a shriek when the wind was stronger.

Grinning in relief, Jeff climbed down and went back to Beany. He explained what he had found.

"Something from another world couldn't be any spookier than that," Beany said.

"I've got an idea, Beany. Terpko is afraid of Bessie's superstitions so he's bound to be afraid of ghosts. Now if we could camp close here and the breeze came up as it usually does some time in the night, we might scare Terpko into telling us where he's been and who he's been talking to."

Beany nodded. "It's a far fetched idea but it might work. It's worth a try. Weren't you figuring on camping here, anyway?"

Jeff nodded. "The wagons will get here too early. The breeze usually goes down about sundown. Can't let Terpko find that Indian and his harp so we'll have to make sure the wagons don't get here till dark. Then we'll have to hope the breeze comes up from this same direction to make the harp play."

"Could climb up and move the harp into the wind if it changes directions," Beany said. "But what if the wind don't blow?"

"Then our plan won't work," Jeff said. "I'll ride back and stop the wagons. You come back about sundown and report that there's a fine place to camp up ahead. I'll order the move."

Beany looked at the trees. "I ain't so taken with the idea of waiting here. But you can bet I'll be back there before it gets dark."

Jeff rode back and halted the wagons a half mile before they reached the big grove of trees. He claimed he saw some harness that needed mending immediately and spent some time on it. The others, especially

Bessie, soon got restless.

"If we don't make camp somewhere, we ain't going to get any supper," she said irritably.

"If I don't get this fixed pretty quick, we'll camp right here," Jeff said.

It wasn't quite sundown when Beany came riding in on his mule and reported a fine place to camp in the trees ahead.

Jeff suddenly finished his work on the harness. "Let's get moving," he ordered.

It was deep twilight when they arrived at the trees. Jeff selected a campsite close to the tree with the Indian corpse and harp. As it usually did here on the prairie, the breeze had gone down with the sun. It was very still now. He hoped the night breeze would spring up in an hour or so.

As if in reply to his request, the first puff of the night breeze touched his face just as they were finishing supper by the light of the campfire. Jeff got up and went over to Toni and Cheery, motioning them to one side. He wasn't sure they would come but they followed him without question.

"I can use a little help," he said. "I think Hod Terpko is up to some mischief. He rode out from our camp yesterday afternoon and won't tell where he went or who he saw. We might scare him into talking tonight if you'll help put the fear in him."

"How can anybody scare him?" Cheery asked.

"He's afraid of Bessie's superstitions," Jeff said. "So he's sure to be scared of ghosts. There's going to be some terrible moaning and shrieking here if the wind gets a little stronger. Toni, didn't someone say you could put on a good act as a medium?"

"I've done it for a joke at parties," Toni said. "I'm not a medium."

"I don't want a real one," Jeff said. He explained about the Indian burials and the harp on the platform with the one Indian. "When that harp gets to moaning, a medium calling up a spirit should get Terpko's attention. Say something to make him think a ghost is out to get him."

"And I'll be the ghost," Cheery added excitedly.

"You're ahead of me," Jeff said, grinning. "But that's the idea. Are you game?"

"Sure," Cheery said, "if I don't have to get too close to that dead Indian."

"You can float in from any direction," Jeff said. "Toni?"

"I'll try," Toni said.

Jeff turned back to the camp. Terpko was scowling at Jeff as he came close to the fire.

"A mighty poor place to camp if there are any Indians around," Terpko grumbled. "They could sneak in through those trees and scalp us before we knew they were there."

"The only Indians in these trees are dead ones," Beany said. "This is their graveyard."

"Dead ones?" Terpko exclaimed. "Why did you set up camp in a graveyard?"

"Live Indians don't go near dead ones at night," Jeff explained. "We're safer here than anywhere."

A low moan came from the trees as the breeze

increased. Jeff glanced at Toni and she sat down cross-legged a short distance from the fire. No one paid any attention to her now but Jeff knew they soon would.

Bessie looked at the trees, just a black mass against the darkening sky, then back at Jeff and Beany. "If this is your idea of a joke, I don't think it's so funny."

"It's no joke," Beany said. "Live Indians won't come near their graveyard at night."

"The only thing we have to worry about is their ghosts," Jeff added softly.

"You shut your trap about ghosts!" Bessie snorted. "The signs have been against us all day as it is."

Toni began moving softly and rocking her shoulders back and forth. Bessie turned troubled eyes on her. "What's wrong with you?" she demanded.

"Must be that supper you cooked," Beany said.

"I feel a presence coming from another world," Toni said in a high monotone.

Beany nudged Jeff. "Is she one of those ghost talkers?"

"So I've heard." He turned to Bessie. "Does she go into a trance often?"

"Not while I'm around," Bessie snorted. "I'll slap her out of it."

Jeff caught Bessie as she started toward Toni. "Let her alone. Don't you know it's the worst kind of luck to molest a medium when she's in a trance? Every ghost she's dreaming up will haunt you for weeks."

Bessie backed off like she'd stepped into a nest of snakes. "I didn't know that. Why in tarnation did she have to pick this place to have a trance?"

"Maybe because it is the place where ghosts hang out," Jeff suggested.

He watched Terpko. He was listening to every word but he wasn't saying anything. Suddenly the breeze picked up sharply and the moan came louder from the trees and Bessie and Terpko backed to the far side of the fire. Beany looked at Jeff then at Toni and nodded as he understood that Toni was part of the act.

"I see a man coming from a long way off. He has a message." Toni's voice held its monotone.

Every eye switched back to her. But a lift in the breeze sent the moan of the harp into a low shriek. Lily screamed and backed off behind Bessie.

"Better move, Lily," Bessie warned, her eyes on the trees. "If I have to run, you'll just be a bump in my road."

"You're not afraid to die, are you, Bessie?" Beany asked.

"Not when the time comes," Bessie said. "But ain't the time nor the place."

The wind increased and the harp shrieked louder. Bessie backed up and Lily retreated quickly to keep from getting stepped on. Toni spoke again, her voice rising to make herself heard.

"The spirit says there is a man here who is evil. He says he will take him away so no harm will come to us."

"Wh-who is the spirit talking about?" Bessie asked, her voice shriller than Toni's.

"He's a tall man. He's been with the wagons for the whole trip."

Jeff watched Terpko. There was no mistaking the effect this was having on him. Nor was there any doubt in anyone's mind that Toni was talking about Terpko.

The wind dropped and the shriek lowered to a wail but then it increased to a shriek again. Just then, Jeff spotted Cheery coming slowly from the trees, although not from the direction of the harp. She had found a sheet and wrapped it around her. In the darkness, she looked more like a ghost than a real ghost would, Jeff thought. He even felt a chill.

"He says he will take the evil man away," Toni repeated in a louder voice.

Bessie threw up her hand and screamed. "May the saints save us!" she shrieked. "There he comes. He'll kill us all."

She wheeled to run but Lily was blocking her way. "I warned you to keep clear," Bessie roared, shoving her aside. "I'm leaving."

"Wait for me!" Beany yelled.

"Beany!" Jeff snapped. "You stay here. I may need you." He turned on Bessie. "Bessie, stop! We'll stand a better chance if we stick together."

"Stick together or fall apart, what difference does it make?" Bessie wailed but she halted her flight. "What a way to die!"

Jeff turned his attention back to Terpko. This whole scheme would be a failure if he didn't break. But Terpko had taken all he could. With a low wail, he turned to run but Jeff was blocking his path.

"Stay here and face the music," Jeff said.

"If that's music," Beany said, shaken in spite of knowing what was making the moans and shrieks, "then I'm tone deaf."

Now there was another moan added to the scream of the harp. Cheery was getting into the mood of her role by adding her own version of a ghostly moan. It was enough to break the nerves of a stronger man than Terpko.

Terpko backed away from Cheery who was between the trees and the campfire now, still at a distance that let the darkness give her an unearthly look. She seemed to be floating just above the ground, the breeze rippling the sheet gracefully. Jeff doubted, however, if anyone else watching was appreciating the gracefulness of the movements.

Terpko wheeled away from the ghost and tried to dodge past Jeff but Jeff reached out a foot and tripped him then fell on him as he tried to scramble up. Beany seemed to come out of the trance he'd fallen into while watching Cheery and plopped his hundred and ninety pounds down on Terpko, too.

"What does that ghost mean by saying he's coming to take you away?" Jeff demanded.

"You got to protect me," Terpko babbled. "I got to shoot that ghost."

"You can't stop a ghost with a gun," Jeff said, grabbing Terpko's hand as he clawed for his gun. "Your only chance is to admit what you planned to do."

"No," Terpko screamed. "Let me go."

"I'm going to hold you for that ghost," Jeff said, although he wasn't at all sure he and Beany could hold

Terpko. He seemed to have superhuman strength as he fought to get away.

Then suddenly all the fight seemed to drain out of Terpko and he began to quiver like a slab of jelly. "All r-r-right. Just keep him from getting me."

"Talk fast," Jeff said. "I can't fight a ghost."

In a high quivering voice that seemed to come from nowhere, Cheery half screamed, "I want Terpko."

If there had been any resistance left in Terpko, that smothered it. But it also drove all reason out of Bessie's head. She wheeled, stumbled over Beany and sprawled on top of Terpko.

"You idiot!" Bessie screamed. "Get out of my way."

"I'd sure like to," Beany said, scrambling away. "I'd like to stay that way, too."

Bessie clawed her way past Terpko, digging some grunts out of him with her boots. She finally got up, looking and sounding more like an agitated buffalo than a woman. Lily was a step ahead of Bessie as they ran to the wagon where Posey and Star had already taken refuge. Jeff turned his attention back to Terpko.

"That ghost is just on the other side of the fire. You'd better talk fast."

"Ross Grilli made me do it," Terpko babbled.

"You work for him?" Jeff asked. Putting one hand behind him, he waved Cheery back.

"He's a friend," Terpko said. "Offered me a slice of something good," Terpko muttered.

Either Terpko had retained enough of his reason to realize that he dare not tell Jeff what Grilli had in mind or else he was so far gone that he couldn't think straight. He kept repeating, "Something good," like a mindless robot.

"If I keep the ghost away from you, what will you do?"

"Go home," Terpko almost sobbed. "Kansas City."

Jeff checked behind him. Cheery had faded back into the trees. The wind still moaned through the harp but it didn't seem so eerie without the ghost out there close to the trees. Bessie was coming slowly back from the wagon and Toni was standing up now, trying to look as if she didn't know what had happened. Jeff nodded to Beany and they got off Terpko but Jeff still held his arm.

"Now you get out of here and don't let any of us ever see you again," he ordered.

Terpko nodded and looked toward the trees. Seeing no ghost, he took a deep breath and started toward the horses, his head swiveling like an owl to make sure no ghost sneaked up on his blind side.

Bessie followed him to the edge of the light cast by the fire. "I'm putting a curse on you," she yelled into the darkness. "If you ever come back, I'll see to it that ghost gets you for sure." She whirled on Jeff. "What's the meaning of all this screeching and wailing and ghosts?"

Jeff explained while Bessie and the girls at the wagon listened.

"You should have beefed Terpko while you had the chance," Beany said.

Bessie agreed. "Turning a snake like that loose is just inviting trouble."

125

"He's pretty well spooked," Jeff said. "He may go where he say he will."

"He probably thinks he's already been in Satan's kitchen," Beany said. "All he needed was a hot fire. Too bad we didn't build that under him."

"I hope he goes to Halifax," Bessie said. "Kansas City is too close."

Jeff was wondering if he might not go to Grilli instead of Kansas City. That would mean bad trouble for Jeff.

XII

As the sound of Terpko's horse faded to the east, Beany shook his head. "He's going east now but that's no guarantee he won't turn around."

"Maybe," Jeff said. "But that ghost was west of camp, remember. He didn't seem too infatuated with that spook."

"Speaking of that ghost," Beany said, "who was that? I know you put somebody up to it."

"Are you talking about me?" Cheery said, coming into the firelight with the sheet draped over her arm.

"You couldn't have looked more like a ghost if you'd been dead a hundred years," Beany said.

"I ought to put arsenic in your soup," Bessie said, glaring at Jeff. "Why didn't you tell us ahead of time what you were up to?"

"If you tell a secret, it's no secret," Jeff said.

He offered to take the girls and Bessie out to see the

harp in the tree. But there were no takers.

"I like my ghosts better in the daytime," Toni said. "I wasn't quite sure whether that was Cheery I saw or something I had dreamed up."

The camp settled downn but Jeff doubted if anyone slept until the wind quieted and the harp stopped moaning. It was a weary camp the next morning as Jeff prepared to move the wagons out. He hoped to get as far as the Cheyene Wells over in Colorado Territory by nightfall.

Jeff's first problem was to find someone to drive Terpko's wagon. He looked at Beany and the short puncher sighed.

"I reckon I can drive," he said. "I've sure done plenty of it in my time."

"How about letting me drive some?" Lily asked. "I've driven a team on buggies and spring wagons. I can handle a wagon."

"Lady, you just got yourself a job," Beany said. "I don't want to neglect Angel too long at a time so you can spell me on the wagon."

"You'd just rather sit on a mule than on a wagon seat where you'd have to work," Bessie snorted.

The wagons moved out with Beany driving the wagon Terpko had handled. Jeff rode well in front. The day was bright and cloudless. Jeff couldn't help thinking about Terpko. Had he gone back to Kansas City? It would be a long trip by himself, all the way across Kansas. If he was a friend of Ross Grilli as he said, it would be much closer to Abe Ryan's ranch where Grilli worked. The trip was almost over for Jeff but his problems seemed to be multiplying instead of resolving. He doubted if Zorn had left the trail. And Jeff would run into Grilli somewhere.

Jeff dropped back to the wagons for dinner then rode forward again. He saw a wisp of smoke off to the right before he'd gone half a mile from the wagons. Reining that way, he approached the spot cautiously. Smoke on a dry prairie was not something to dismiss lightly.

The smoke dissipated before he got close enough to pinpoint its location. Jeff moved cautiously. That could have been a cooking fire built by Terpko or Zorn.

When he finally located the ashes of the fire in a little draw, there was no one near. He examined the ashes, finding them still warm. The fire had been built only a few feet from some prairie grass which would have ignited if a spark had touched it. The men who built this fire were not prairie men, Jeff decided, and there had been two or three of them.

Jeff kept a keen watch for sight of the men through the afternoon but saw nothing. He arrived at the Cheyenne Wells a little before camping time. The first well had been dug here about 1860 by Lt. Fitch's surveying party trying to lay out a road from the Missouri to the gold fields at Denver. It had been all but abandoned because of the War but had been revived and used again when a new survey established the Butterfield Overland Despatch in 1865. Now this part of the road was abandoned by regular traffic. There were still a few wagons on the road, however, such as these Jeff was guiding.

Jeff had the campsite picked out when the wagons

rolled in. It was on the north side of the creek, which was dry except for some pools in deep potholes. There were old campsites on both banks of the creek. The well was shored up by heavy planks standing vertically around the perimeter of the well. It was only a few feet to water but when the holes in the river were dry, that water was most welcome to travelers.

Bessie had the campfire going and the pot of stew on by sundown. It had been a hot day and Beany, who usually wore a bandanna around the neck, had taken it off and stuffed it into his hip pocket.

Jeff saw trouble suddenly loom up when Beany went over to the fire to check on supper, a procedure he repeated faithfully every evening. It usually brought an outburst from Bessie but Jeff guessed she would think he wasn't hungry if he failed to check out supper while it was cooking.

Tonight, however, that bandanna of Beany's was dangling out of his hip pocket and waving back and forth as he walked. Jeff wasn't the first to notice it. Hercules was already preparing to do something about that dangling flag.

The goat was about fifteen feet behind Beany. Rearing up on his legs, he shook his head angrily, his beard flipping back and forth. Jeff shouted a warning but the goat was already charging.

Beany was bent over the pot checking it. It wasn't even hot yet, the fire having just been started.

Hercules' aim was perfect. He hit the flag in Beany's pocket squarely. Beany's grunt could have been heard in all the wagons. His head barely missed going into the kettle. He sprawled over the iron kettle, upsetting it and spilling the contents onto the fire and beyond. The fire sputtered and went out. Beany rolled off the hot coals and came up cursing like a dull whacker.

Bessie ignored Beany's language and used some choice adjectives of her own. "Now look what you done, you inquisitive old polecat!" she screamed.

"Look what *I've* done?" Beany roared. "It's that ding-busted goat." He tried to brush himself off but there was stew mixed with the dust on his clothes. It made a savory mud.

"If you didn't have to smell everything like a dog, you wouldn't have had your beak in that kettle," Bessie yelled, picking up the kettle and staring inside. She gave it a swish and threw what was left at Beany.

"Hey, that's our supper," Posey yelled from the wagon.

"Do you want to eat it after Old Blunder-foot has been swimming in it?" Bessie shot back.

"I wasn't swimming," Beany roared. "That ding-busted goat tried to drown me in that stew."

"Too bad he didn't make it work," Bessie snorted. "I wish he had more brains instead of so much butting power."

"He ain't got room for brains. His head is solid concrete."

"He's got more brains than you," Bessie snapped. "So where does that put you?"

"In the mood to kill a goat and a certain female with a tongue like a bull whip and the brain of a bumblebee."

Beany glared at Bessie, then at the goat but neither showed any inclination to test his restraint further. Star came running over and took Hercules by the horns and led him back to the wagon.

"Too bad some people can't be put in their place that easy," Beany muttered.

Jeff promised Beany that he'd be back in time for the third watch and rode out after explaining about the campfire he'd found this afternoon. Beany was too preoccupied with getting the stew off his clothes to ask questions.

Guessing that men who were careless enough to build a dinner fire that gave off visible smoke would also be careless in selecting a night camp, Jeff headed northwest. They were probably camped somewhere out there a little ahead of the wagons and off the road.

Guiding his horse toward the highest knoll he could see against the darkening sky, he reined up and scanned the horizon. Down in a gully, not as far away as he had expected, he saw the flicker of a small campfire. Jeff rode cautiously toward it. On the opposite side of a ridge from the fire, he dismounted and ground-hitched his horse. Moving to the top of the knoll, he dropped to his hands and knees.

He was more than just surprised at what he saw. There were four men, apparently secure in the belief that no one from the wagons would dare come looking for them even if their presence was suspected. Jeff frowned as he recognized Ross Grilli across the fire facing him. Grilli should know better than to build a fire at night if he wanted to keep his location hidden.

Jeff wasn't surprised at seeing Terpko and Zorn. Somehow he had expected both men to stay around and Terpko had said he was working for Grilli. But he was totally surprised at the fourth man, Orrin Ivie. He had been sure he had seen the last of the man from Kansas City.

Jeff watched them for a while. They seemed relaxed and full of conversation. He considered surprising them. But he knew that would be foolhardy. Zorn was a gunman; he'd react instantly to surprise. Grilli was not one to be immobilized by surprise, either. The odds were too great. He headed back to the wagons to prepare a defense against the attack he expected would come.

Jeff got another surprise when he reached camp. He had expected to find everyone asleep except Norrie on guard. But they were awake waiting for him. They gathered near the center wagon as he came into camp.

"What did you find?" Beany asked.

Jeff looked over at the girls gathered around Bessie and Beany. "They're ganging up on us," he said. "I found their camp and even considered blasting them but I didn't like the odds of four to one."

"Who's ganging up on us?" Bessie demanded.

"Hod Terpko and Vinton Zorn. Ross Grilli and Orrin Ivie have joined them."

"Ivie?" Posey broke in. "Didn't he go back to Kansas City?"

Jeff shook his head. "He got his head on the wrong end and came this way. We've got to be on the alert."

"The girls will be ready," Bessie promised. "You saw

how they can shoot. We'll keep our rifles loaded and ready."

"Better try to get some sleep. They might try an Indian tactic and hit at dawn."

Jeff turned away and the others headed back to their blankets. Norrie had not left his guard post. Jeff had barely rolled out his blankets when he saw one of the girls coming from the center wagon. He wasn't surprised when he recognized Posey. He had seen her reaction when he mentioned Ivie's name.

"I want to talk to you," Posey said quietly when she reached him. She glanced at Beany.

"I share everything with Beany," Jeff said. "Is it about Ivie?"

Posey nodded and dropped down on her knees close to Jeff. "Back in Kansas City, I got into an argument with Bud Ivie, Orrin's brother. He was trying to kill me with a knife when I shot him with my derringer. I didn't mean to kill him but I did. When I was checking to see if he was dead, I found a big roll of money. He must have robbed a bank or something. Anyway, I thought it was a shame to let all that money go so I took it."

"So you think Orrin Ivie is after that money?" Jeff asked when Posey paused in her story.

"I'm sure of it," Posey said. "He knew Bud and I were together a lot. Part of that money might have been his. At least, he must have known Bud had it with him. And of course, he'll try to kill me to avenge his brother."

Jeff nodded. "No wonder you're afraid of him."

"Does it show?" she asked.

"Enough," Jeff said. "I'm not going to ask how you happened to be with Bud Ivie. That's none of my business. But it is my business to see to it that you get to my uncle's ranch safe and sound."

Posey smiled. "Thanks, Jeff. I had you figured for a square shooter. I don't see many like you in my business."

She rose and disappeared quickly under the middle wagon where her bedroll was spread out.

Jeff turned to Beany. "You still haven't told me why you brought Posey along."

"I told you there was a good reason but I wouldn't tell anybody what it was," Beany said. "Maybe it's time I did. It's Abe's fault. A man in Kansas City borrowed quite a bit of money from Abe when he still lived in Missouri. He's wealthy now so Abe wrote for his money. He said he'd pay it. Abe needs the money bad so I was to get it."

"What's that got to do with Posey?" Jeff asked.

"Posey is the daughter of one of Abe's best friends. Abe is sure that Posey is the Queen of Innocence. So he wrote to Posey and asked her to get the money from this man and have it ready for me. She did. Only she wanted to come along with me instead of just giving me the money."

"I guess you know the reason now why she wanted to come."

Beany nodded. "I sure do. But I didn't then. I didn't even know what kind of a girl she was. I thought Abe would be tickled pink to see the daughter of his old friend so I brought her along. Abe made me swear I wouldn't tell anybody about the money Posey was to give me. Somebody might steal it if word got out I had it."

"Did Posey give you the money?"

Beany shook his head. "Since she was coming along, I let her keep it. Seemed like the safest way to get it there. Who would expect a girl going west to get married to have a lot of money with her?"

"Now she's got Uncle Abe's money and the money she stole from Bud Ivie. That would make quite a haul for Orrin Ivie."

"He won't get it," Beany said savagely.

"We'd better make mighty sure of that," Jeff said. "Posey has suddenly become a very valuable piece of cargo."

Beany went out to take Norrie's place as guard. Jeff rolled into his blankets and tried to sleep. In spite of his worries, he did drop off to sleep and was roused when it was his turn to take the guard.

He was watching carefully as the first streaks of dawn lightened the prairie. Then, off to the north of the big well where the wagons were parked, he caught a movement; he knew instantly it wasn't an Indian. No Indian would be careless enough to let himself be seen like that. It had to be one of the four men from the camp he'd seen last night.

"Roll out," he yelled. "Attack!"

XIII

Jeff ran back to the wagons. The others were out of their blankets by the time he got there. Beany was still in his bare feet but he was gripping his rifle.

"Indians?" he asked, scanning the dark prairie.

"Pale faced Indians," Jeff said.

"Those polecats!" Beany muttered. "We'll burn their britches."

"A couple of you girls get in each wagon," Jeff ordered. "Roll up the canvas just enough to peek out and shoot through. Beany and Norrie and I will get under the wagons. I think they're all to the north of us."

"I'd like to drown them in that well," Bessie yelled. "Lily, you and Toni take the front wagon. Star and Cheery the back one. Posey and me will blister them from here."

Jeff was glad that Bessie was keeping Posey with her. Bessie was as good with a rifle as any man he'd seen. She likely reasoned that Orrin Ivie would be after Posey so she was taking the responsibility of protecting her.

Jeff stationed himself under the middle wagon while Beany took the front one. Norrie crawled under the rear wagon. Jeff expected the attack to come from the north and west. Those men so far hadn't displayed any of the cunning of the plainsmen. Likely they wouldn't try any flanking maneuver in their attack, either.

Beany spotted the first attacker and opened up on

him. The flat plain north of the campsite was long and level before it rose to the first knoll. The attackers had left their horses somewhere behind the knoll and crawled toward the wagons, evidently hoping for surprise to gain their ends. Jeff had ruined that by spotting one of the men. Now they seemed intent on fighting their way into camp.

They opened up with a barrage of bullets. In the dim dawn light, they had gotten close enough to be well within effective rifle range. But there were few visible targets among the wagons.

Jeff quickly spotted the four places from which the rifles were working. They were spread out in a small semi-circle to the north and west. He started shooting at one of the spots and Norrie opened up on another. Then from the wagons a roaring volley peppered the area where the riflemen were. After only a moment, a second volley followed the first.

There was a yell from one of the riflemen in the grass but it sounded to Jeff more like one of alarm than of pain. They evidently hadn't figured on the girls fighting so well but Terpko should have known they would. He had seen them perform during the Indian attack close to Fort Harker. After a few more rifle shots, there was silence on the prairie.

"Fixing to charge us?" Bessie called.

"I doubt it," Jeff guessed. "There are only four of them. There's nine of us. We've got good cover; they haven't. They may be a little short of brains but I figure they're smart enough to see the cards are stacked against them."

"Ought to send that ding-busted goat out after them," Beany muttered.

"They'd kill him before he got ten feet," Norrie said.

"You've got the idea," Beany said. "Only trouble is, there ain't a rifle bullet between here and St. Louis hard enough to crack his skull."

"I have the feeling there's nobody out there now," Jeff said. He backed out from under the wagon and lifted the flap on the center wagon. "See anything out there, Bessie?"

"Can't see hide nor hair of them," Bessie said. "Seems like polecats like them ought to leave a smell even if you can't see them."

Toni called from the front wagon. "I saw one man backing away on his hands and knees."

"Toni hurried him a little with a shot that was just short," Lily added.

"You girls stay in the wagons," Jeff said. "I'm going to make sure they're gone. Beany, you watch that they don't try to circle and come up on our blind side."

"We can't afford to have a blind side." Beany said.

Jeff got his horse and saddled him. If they were retreating, he wanted to give them time to get away before he rode out. Sitting on a horse, he'd be a perfect target if they were still lingering out there.

He mounted and from his seat in the saddle, he scanned the prairie. The sun would be up in a few minutes; the light was strong enough now to reveal anything on the flat bottom land between the creek and the hills to the north. But nothing stirred. Then, as he rode his horse away from the wagons, he caught a glimpse of a man on the hill to the north.

To make sure they were gone, Jeff rode over the area where the man had been and up to the top of the knoll. There was no sign of any of them in the hills. He did see the flattened grass where the four horses had been staked.

Reining around, he headed back to camp. The raiders had been thwarted in this attack. But they might try again. They were surely too smart, however, to try a frontal attack next time. He would have to be on the alert for some kind of trick. He didn't think any of the men had been hurt in their abortive attempt this morning.

Arriving back at the wagons, he called for a report. No one had sustained even a scratch. Bessie and Star started to stir up breakfast while Norrie and Beany brought in buffalo chips from the prairie for the fire. The chips were scarce because there had been too many campers here in recent years.

The attack had delayed the morning chores and it was long after sun-up before the pans were washed and put away and the men had the horses brought in for harnessing. The wind had come up from the northwest, making it difficult to get any heat from the fire and that had delayed breakfast, too. Now the wind suddenly brought in a new threat.

Beany discovered it first. He pointed to the north-west and yelled. "Hey, look over there!"

Jeff needed only one glance to see that this new danger could quickly become a disaster. Prairie fires were nothing uncommon out here but there hadn't been any rain for a few days and the grass, although green, was dry enough to burn. There was also a lot of dead grass from last year still standing among the new green stems. Those dry stems of grass would burn like paper.

"Fire!" Bessie roared like a locomotive whistle. "Let's get hitched up and get out of here."

Jeff directed the work as teams were hastily hitched to the wagons, some almost before the harness was fastened in place. In fact, Norrie forgot to buckle the hame strap on the collar of one of his horses and when he snapped the neckyoke to the harness, the hames slid off the collar and back over the horse's shoulders. The horse, not used to such maneuvers, shied away, sliding the harness even farther but of place.

Jeff rushed over and caught the horse and yelled for Beany to help Norrie untangle the harness and get it buckled in place. It took a while to get the harness unsnarled. When it was buckled tight and the neckyoke back on its snap, the fire had spread in the northwest until it was a semi-circle of flame.

"That's not far away," Bessie yelled. "If anybody else pulls a clinker like that, we'll leave him."

"We can't outrun that fire," Beany said to Jeff. "Look how it's spreading."

"It's getting help in that spreading," Jeff said.

"You mean those chicken-livered varmints set that fire?" Beany exploded.

"Of course," Jeff said. "What else would start a prairie fire this early in the morning with no lightning?"

Jeff had tried to think that even such men as Grilli

and Zorn wouldn't set a fire to burn the wagons and the people in them. But he knew there was no other explanation. The railroad was five or six miles south of here at the little town named Cheyenne Wells that had sprung up along the tracks, so a spark from an engine could not have started it.

An ordinary fire wouldn't spread like this one, either. It would burn straight ahead of the wind, spreading only gradually as it came. This one was sprouting new blazes to the right and left of the center. The new fires quickly burned grass between them and became one wall of fire.

"If we can't outrun it, what do we do?" Norrie asked, his voice thin with fear.

"Let's get the wagons across the creek and south of that big water hole," Jeff shouted.

"The creek ain't got any water; it won't stop that fire," Bessie yelled.

"That deep hole has water. We'll get right south of it. Hurry!"

Just to the west of the water hole, the creek bed was practically dry. It was also sandy. It would take some hard pulling to get a wagon down into the stream bed and up the other bank. But there was no other choice. Whoever had set that fire had made sure that the wind would carry it straight at the wagons, cutting them off from any escape.

Jeff leaped off his horse and helped urge Norrie's team to pull harder as they hit the loose sand in the creek bed. The horses were not warmed up; their collars were cold; they were reluctant to throw all their weight into such a task so soon after being hitched up.

Jeff used his hat to slap the rumps of the horses and Norrie was standing up, lashing them with the ends of the lines. Smoke was already swirling down toward them as the green grass among the dry stems gave off a suffocating smoke.

Norrie's team struggled up the south bank and Jeff motioned him to the east to get on the south bank of the deep pool in the creek. Then he turned back to help the next wagon, the one Bessie was driving: It had the lightest load with only the girls. Beany was on the wagon with the girls' trunks, the heaviest load.

Jeff motioned for Bessie to come but the wagon didn't move. He ran up the bank to the wagon.

"What's holding you up?"

"Star can't get Hercules to come."

"Let the critter burn!" Beany yelled. "The son of Satan ought to be used to fire, anyway."

Jeff ran around the wagon. The two nanny goats were tied to the rear of the wagon and would have to follow. But Hercules was defiantly standing back, bleating his displeasure at the proceedings.

"He'll follow the nannies," Jeff yelled at Star.

"I don't think he will," Star shouted. "He don't like water."

"There's not enough water in that creek to wet his hoofs," Jeff yelled in irritation. "He'll come if it gets down to that or singeing his hair."

"I wish it would get hot enough to singe his heart," Beany howled. "Get that wagon moving so I can get across."

Star had Hercules by the horns now, the way she had trained him to lead. But he was balking. Jeff got behind the goat and pushed. The goat braced his feet but he was no match for Jeff, especially in the mood Jeff was in now.

Hercules bleated angrily with every step and when they reached the wagon, he planted his feet firmly. Jeff saw no rope to tie him to the wagon.

"Get in the wagon," he shouted at Star and grabbed the goat by one horn and a back leg like he would a calf being thrown at a branding fire and heaved him into the wagon before the goat could muster a protest.

"You'll hurt him!" Star yelled.

"He won't hurt him enough unless he kills him," Beany shouted. "Get that goat crate out of my way."

"You watch what you're calling a goat crate!" Bessie shouted back.

But she slapped the reins and put the team into the sandy creek bed. With a few desperate lunges, the team jerked the wagon down into the creek bed, through the sandy bottom, and up the far bank.

Jeff wheeled to help Beany who already had his team moving. The fire was getting close enough now that the smoke was beginning to choke Jeff and he could feel the heat. The wind was whipping it toward them in a blinding rush.

Beany's team just couldn't pull the wagon up the far side of the creek. Jeff ran over to Norrie's wagon, grabbed a chain out of the back and called for Norrie to bring his team. By the time Jeff had the chain fastened to the iron loop in the end of the tongue, Norrie had the team backed into place up on the bank of the creek. Jeff fastened the tugs of Norrie's horses to the chain and gave the signal.

Beany and Norrie both yelled at the horses and Jeff threw his weight against the rear wheel of the wagon. He discovered that Bessie and all the girls were in the creek, too, pushing on the wagon box and trying to turn the wheels. With this additional help, the wagon rolled through the sand and up the far bank.

When all the wagons were south of the pool, Jeff put everyone to work with every bucket they had, carrying water from the pool and wetting the horses and wagons and the grass out as far as they could from the wagons. It was slow, hard work because the cliff above the pool was vertical and the path to and from the pool was a long switchback up which the water had to be carried.

When the heat from the fire got too intense and the smoke too thick, Jeff called them all together on the south side of the wagons.

The fire reached the pool of water and stopped. On either side of the pool, it jumped the creek bed and caught the dead reeds and grass on the other side and raced up the south bank. But it sputtered and died when it tried to move toward the wagons. The wet grass would not burn.

In ten minutes, the worst of the fire was past. Only buffalo chips and old sticks of wood left by campers were smoldering on the blackened prairie.

"They'll come after us now since we weren't burned in the fire," Jeff said. "Get your guns."

No one had to be told twice. Even the girls gingerly

144

picked up the rifles which were hot from the fire that had swept past. Jeff scanned the hills to the northwest and was rewarded by the sight of four riders urging their reluctant horses over the black prairie.

"When they get close enough, drop some bullets in front of those horses," Jeff said. "They're already riled up from having to go over hot ground."

The riders kept coming, apparently expecting the people at the wagons to be so demoralized by the fire that they wouldn't be watching for more trouble. When Jeff gave the word, all nine rifles opened up in one volley. Bullets kicked up black ashes all around the horses.

It was too much for the skittish animals. One erupted in a bucking spasm and the others seemed to catch the fever from him. In a minute, it was a bucking free-for-all there on the burned-over prairie. Only one rider, Ross Grilli, stayed in the saddle. The others, not used to sitting on the hurricane deck of a bucking horse, sprawled on the hot embers of the recent fire. Their howls carried to those at the wagons.

Bessie emptied her rifle around the loose horses, sending them racing back toward the hills. "Let those two-legged fire-bugs walk on that hot ground," she shouted in glee. "Maybe that will burn some of the meanness out of them."

Jeff grinned for the first time in hours as he watched the three men hopping back toward the hills like frozen-footed roosters.

When they were gone, Norrie reported that he had some broken harness, caused by not getting it buckled on right, despite the help the others had so unselfishly given him. Jeff wasn't surprised but he didn't condemn Norrie for making the mistake. It had been a furious few minutes when they were trying to get the wagons across the creek to safety.

They started work on the harness. Jeff noted that the fire had gone more east than south. It would miss the settlement of Cheyenne Wells. He didn't know how far it would burn before it ran into a creek big enough to halt it.

It was late afternoon before the harness was fixed and the wagons ready to travel again.

"We'll stay right here tonight," Jeff decided. "It's a dry run from here to Kit Carson. We've got water here so we'll load up before we start early tomorrow morning."

There were no objections from the others. They'd had enough work and excitement for one day. As soon as the sun went down, Jeff saddled his horse, telling Beany he was going to scout around and see if the four men were really gone. Even considering their two failures to take the wagons today, he wasn't sure they wouldn't try again.

The ground was cool where the fire had raced over it. Only an occasional buffalo chip still smoldered, sending up a plume of smoke in the now still air.

If the four were still here, they would be beyond the burned area where there would be grass for their horses. All the camp had for grass was in the triangle that the fire had left when it went around the water hole. That would be enough for tonight.

Beyond the burned area, Jeff rode into the hills. Feeling sure the men would have a campfire if they were still around, he rode to the top of the knoll to get a better view of the surrounding country. He knew he was silhouetted against the night sky but it was the only way he was going to see the country around him.

Suddenly he felt a tug at his shoulder followed by the spang of a rifle. With a shock, he realized that some marksman had his silhouette in his sights.

XIV

Jeff's first instinct was to dive off the horse. But then he realized he'd be grounded and the marksman could move in for a better shot. He wanted to get to that man, anyway.

Throwing himself forward on his horse, he kicked him into a run straight at the spot where he'd seen the flash of the marksman's rifle.

Jeff expected at least one more shot before he reached the ambusher but there was none. Then, above the pounding of his horse's feet, he heard the thunder of another running horse. That horse was angling off to the east and Jeff reined his horse in pursuit. The gunman evidently had no stomach for a hand to hand fight; ambush was more to his liking. That could fit any of the men who had started that fire today.

After a short run, Jeff pulled up his horse to listen. The sound of drumming hoofbeats was still ahead but

Jeff was losing ground. He nudged his horse into a run again. The rider ahead seemed to be riding in a big circle for he was already out on the burned area. Why was he riding this way? Surely his camp was in the other direction.

When Jeff reined up again to listen, there was no sound ahead. He turned his head both ways, listening so hard that it seemed he heard a roar all around him.

With a sigh, Jeff turned back toward camp. He had lost the ambusher. It really didn't make any difference which one of the four men it was. He had hoped to catch him and put him out of action since he'd decided that the only way he was going to get to his uncle's ranch safely was to get rid of the four men hounding his trail.

It took Jeff a while to get his bearings. When he hit the creek, he realized he was east of the water hole. He reined to the west. The late moon came up, throwing some light over the prairie.

Before long, he brought the white canvas tops of the wagons into view. The campfire was out. It was Norrie who challenged Jeff as he rode in. Jeff identified himself.

"Everything quiet here?" he asked.

"Has been," Norrie said. "Somebody's stirring in camp now but I ain't about to poke around to find out who it is."

Jeff grinned. "Might be Bessie."

Norrie nodded. "If it was, I'd get my ears beat off for prying."

"I've got big ears," Jeff said. "I'll do the prying.

Can't imagine why anybody would be moving around now unless somebody's sick."

Jeff dismounted and unsaddled, staking out his horse. He listened intently but didn't hear any sounds from the camp. Probably whoever had made the noise had gone back to bed. Norrie was alert, at least, to have noticed the stirring in camp.

Jeff was half way from his horse to the wagons when he heard a roar ahead. He recognized Bessie's bellow.

He broke into a run toward the wagons. He saw Bessie, nightgown flapping as she run around the wagon.

"What's the wrong?" Jeff yelled.

"Somebody stole Posey's money," Bessie yelled back.

Jeff didn't suppose that Bessie knew about Posey's money. Who else knew about it except Orrin Ivie? Was Ivie in the camp?

As Jeff got closer, he saw a man run past a wagon and turn behind the rear vehicle. He heard him yell and he realized that he must have tripped over the tether ropes of the two nanny goats that Star always staked out behind the rear wagon when they camped.

"Who is it?" he yelled at Bessie as he raced toward the rear wagon.

"Don't know," Bessie panted. "But I'll skin him alive if I catch him."

Jeff reached the rear of the wagon just as the man scrambled to his feet. The two nanny goats were jerking against their ropes and bleating in terror. Hercules, who had been some distance from the wagons, came running in response to the frightened bleats of the nannies.

Jeff was close enough then to recognize Vinton Zorn. It must have been Zorn who had ambushed him tonight; then, when Jeff gave chase, he had cut back to the camp to get Posey's money. Orrin Ivie had probably told him about it.

Jeff raced out around the nanny goats, not wanting to be tripped by those ropes like Zorn had been. But before he could get close to Zorn, Hercules had taken a part in the melee. From his angry bleat, Jeff guessed he had recognized Zorn.

Jeff slowed down. Hercules would keep Zorn occupied until Jeff could get close enough to take a hand. Zorn apparently recognized his danger and feared the goat more than he did the wrath of those in the wagons.

With a yell of terror, apparently forgetting his gun, he wheeled and raced away from the wagons with Hercules only a few jumps behind and gaining with every leap. Jeff broke into a hard run again. At the rate Zorn was going, it would take Jeff a while to catch him.

Zorn had run north from the wagons, straight toward the water hole from which Jeff and the others had carried water earlier to dampen the wagons and surrounding grass to keep the fire from reaching them. There was a path from the prairie level down a slope to the west then back to the water level. But directly ahead of Zorn was a sharp drop-off. He either didn't know about it or, in his panic, had forgotten about it.

He saw it just before reaching the edge. He stopped and wheeled to face the goat. Hercules didn't stop. He seemed pleased that his target had halted and posed for him. Hercules drilled his hard head into Zorn's stomach, bringing an explosion of breath from the gunman. Hercules stopped to observe the effect of his hit. Zorn didn't stop. The force of Hercules' blow sent him reeling backward, almost flying through the air. He didn't have a chance to get his feet on the ground before he went over the edge of the cliff.

Jeff ran to the top of the cliff and stood not far from Hercules, peering over and listening. After a few dislodged rocks rattled to a stop, there was an eerie silence from below.

"Bring a lantern," he yelled back at the camp which was fully awake now.

Beany brought the lantern while Bessie and the girls gathered at the top of the cliff. Posey had lost her composure for once, showing more agitation than she had let anyone see since they'd left Kansas City.

Jeff took the lantern from Beany and ran along the edge of the cliff to the path that wound down the slope to the water. Beany was only a step behind him. It was quite a distance down to the water level. Jeff had thought it was a long way when they'd been carrying buckets of water up from the water hole during the fire. It didn't seem any shorter now.

"Is it that gunman?" Beany panted.

"Yeah," Jeff said. Thinking of Zorn's attempts to get him into a gun battle, Jeff pulled his gun out of the holster as he reached the bottom of the path. Zorn might be hurt but an injured rattler was even more dangerous than a healthy one.

They stopped short of the rocks. Jeff set the lantern on a rock then moved ahead, well out of the light thrown by the lantern. He made too good a target carrying it.

He found Zorn crumpled at the foot of the cliff, directly beneath the spot where he had fallen. Jeff approached him cautiously but when he got closer, he saw the odd cant of his head. He had landed on the rocks in such a way that his neck had been broken.

"Dead," he reported to Beany who brought the lantern forward.

"Posey's money?" Beany asked.

Jeff found a sack just a few inches from Zorn's outstretched hand. That helped explain why Zorn hadn't used his gun on the goat. Panic had likely had a part but Zorn would have been forced to drop the money sack to get his gun. And he'd had no intention of losing that money.

"I won't let it out of my sight again," she promised.

"He broke his neck in the fall," Jeff reported to the others. "We'll bury him in the morning before we move on."

Jeff couldn't sleep even when he wasn't on guard duty. Zorn had tried to ambush him tonight. Grilli and Terpko would try to kill him before he got to Abe Ryan's ranch. And the money would not be safe until Orrin Ivie was dead or chased back to Kansas City. The only way he was going to get this train through was to eliminate those three threats.

While Bessie and Star were starting breakfast during the dawn hour, Jeff asked Posey if she had a small solid box. She didn't ask why he wanted it but dug into her trunk and came up with a jewelry box from which she took a handful of cheap, gaudy jewelry.

Jeff examined the box and nodded his approval. "We'll put the money in this and nail it to the underside of the wagon," he said. "If it is close to the back standard, it might not be noticed even if somebody looks under the wagon."

"Good idea," Posey agreed. "We'd better nail the lid shut before we nail it to the wagon box."

Jeff nodded and put the money inside. It filled the box. Nailing the lid shut, he slid under the wagon and nailed the box securely to the wagon bed. Even the roughest roads shouldn't loosen those nails. The risk of losing it off the wagon was smaller than leaving it where any of the three men waiting for them could find it. Ivie had apparently told the others about the money or Zorn wouldn't have known about it.

Breakfast over, while the others were hitching up, Jeff rode out to look for Zorn's companions. In the daylight, he found their camp easily enough. He hadn't quite reached it last night when Zorn ambushed him. The coals of the fire were still hot but the tracks headed west and the horses had been moving rapidly. They weren't hanging around any longer, matching their pace to that of the wagons.

Jeff's first thought was of Abe Ryan's ranch. Whatever mischief Grilli had planned for Abe was about to be instigated, Jeff guessed. After that, they would come back and meet the wagons. There would probably be time for both because the riders could cover the ground much faster than the wagons.

He turned back to the wagons and was surprised to find they hadn't moved far. Beany was faunching mad. He and Norrie had buried Zorn then Star had discovered that one of her nanny goats had gotten loose. Apparently when Zorn tripped over the ropes the night before, had loosened a picket pin. It had taken almost an hour to capture the nanny goat who was enjoying her new-found freedom.

"We've got to get to Uncle Abe's fast," Jeff told Beany. "I think all three thieves are heading that way."

Beany frowned. "They must have spooked when Zorn didn't come back. He was probably the best gun slinger in the bunch."

"Grilli is no slouch," Jeff said. "I've got to get to Uncle Abe and put a stop to whatever Grilli has in mind."

Jeff and Beany were in front of wagons which were just ready to move out. Samson was at the heels of Beany's mule, Angel. Jeff saw Hercules coming toward them from the rear wagon. He appeared as angry as a bee from an upset hive.

"Watch that goat," he warned Beany.

"That son of Satan helped keep that nanny goat running so we couldn't catch her. He didn't like it when we caught that nanny and tied her to the wagon again."

"He's not happy yet," Jeff said.

Samson apparently sensed the goat's mood. He growled and turned to face Hercules. The goat came on, breaking into a run as he got nearer. Samson didn't retreat.

When the goat was within a few feet, Samson dived at his heels. The goat bleated and wheeled on the dog. Three whirls later both the dog and goat were almost underneath Angel. The mule tolerated the noise but when the goat's horns brushed his belly, he suddenly kicked up his heels. It wasn't a real bucking exhibition but it caught Beany by surprise. He lost his grip and slid over the mule's head.

Beany's yell when he landed did more to break up the fight than any physical interference could have done. Hercules headed back for the wagons on the run. Samson started after him then thought better of it and turned back to the mule.

Jeff dismounted and hurried to Beany who was getting up gingerly. Then Jeff saw the reason for the howl. Beany had landed squarely on a prickly pear cactus. Some of those long spines had stuck in him.

Jeff helped him to his feet. "We'll have to get those thorns out."

"How?" Beany sputtered. "I can't see back there."

"I can," Bessie said positively, coming from the wagons to see what the uproar was about. "Get that saddle off the mule and put it down here. Then you lean over it and strip off those britches."

"What?" Beany roared. "Right out here in front of everybody?"

"We ain't got no doctor's private office to work in," Bessie snorted.

"Ain't no woman going to pick stickers out of my seat," Beany yelled.

"Then ride all the way to the mountains with them

stickers," Bessie said.

Beany looked at Jeff. Jeff shook his head. "She's a lot better at pulling stickers than I am. Better get those britches off. She can't pull them if she can't see them."

Beany swore and raged until there were in his eyes, a mixture of pain, fury and embarrassment. But he lowered his pants and leaned over the saddle. Bessie wasted no motions in getting to work on the thorns that stuck out like pins in a pin cushion. The girls stood back at the wagon, pity for Beany's pain in their faces. But it couldn't hold down the giggles at his embarrassment.

"I'm going to catch that goat someday," Beany muttered between yells as Bessie pulled the thorns, "and I'm going to tie him in the middle of the biggest cactus bed I can find then throw ten thousand mad ants all over him."

When the job was done and Beany was presentable again, Jeff called him aside and hit him with a proposal that pushed the pain of the thorns from his mind.

"I've got to catch Grilli and those other two before they get to Uncle Abe. I'm going to ride after them. You can handle the wagons till I get back, can't you?"

Beany frowned. "I reckon I can try. But if anything happens, you know what Abe will do because you left your job."

"I figure my job is to keep Uncle Abe alive and maybe save his ranch. I don't know what Grilli is up to."

Beany nodded and Jeff reined around and rode to the

west before Beany could think of another argument to keep him here.

Jeff rode to the camp he'd located this morning and picked up the trail. The men had been traveling fast so they had a good start on him. It would take him a while to catch them if they kept up that pace.

For several hours, he followed the tracks. They seemed to be making no effort to hide them. Apparently they hadn't expected anyone to try to trail them. They had been the hunters all the way; they hadn't expected to be the hunted.

Jeff kept a close watch ahead. He wanted to see them before they saw him. The tracks showed that he wasn't gaining much on them, however. At this rate, they'd get to Abe's ranch before he could. And they might do the damage they had in mind, whatever that was.

Then, some time after noon, the tracks separated. One set went straight ahead but the other two swung to the north. He thought of following the one set; those tracks were going toward Abe's ranch. But where were the other two going? Something warned him that he'd better find out.

Reining to the right on the trail of the two, he followed at a trot. It was not hard to follow until the tracks took to some buffalo grass matted so thickly that there was no sand or dirt showing. Here the tracking was much slower.

The tracks finally turned into a gully that ran northeast and when they came out of that they were headed almost due east. It hit Jeff suddenly where these two riders were going. Back to the wagons!

He had been suckered into a trap. They had guessed he would follow them if they headed fast toward Abe Ryan's ranch. But only one, probably Grilli, had gone on to the ranch. That left Terpko and Ivie to go back to the wagons. Ivie wanted that money and probably revenge on Posey. Terpko had likely been promised a share of the money for helping. They would expect Jeff to be gone.

He was gone and it was his own fault. Beany had told him he should stay with the wagons. He kicked his horse into a gallop. But he knew he was too far behind the two to catch them before they got to the wagons.

XV

As he urged his horse back toward the wagons, Jeff's mind turned to those in the train, particularly Toni. Terpko had wanted Toni and had tried to court her. Jeff had fought him over that. He wouldn't be there to fight him when Terpko got there this time.

Reason caught up with Jeff after a couple of miles of hard riding. If he didn't slow down, he'd run his horse into the ground. He reined the horse down to a trot. He had lost the trail of the two but he didn't care about that now. If they didn't go to the wagons, he'd be very happy. If they did, the quickest way he could get there would be the direct route, ignoring the trail.

Well before dark, he cut south to the old B. O. D. trail. He knew Beany would bring the wagons along the trail. As long as he stayed in it, he wouldn't miss the wagons. Darkness caught up with him before he brought them into sight.

He wished there were more wagon trains on the trail. But they were still some distance from the end of the railroad. The stage coaches and the freighters ran only from the end of track into Denver.

Jeff began to wonder if he had somehow missed the wagons as the night wore on and he kept his horse at the ground eating trot. He should have met the train where it camped. It would be a dry camp because they were crossing the divide between the Smoky Hill River and the Big Sandy.

Many things worked their way into Jeff's mind. His biggest worry was that Terpko and Ivie had captured the wagons and had turned them off the main trail so that Jeff couldn't find them. Terpko and Ivie wanted the money and once they found that Ivie had taken his revenge against Posey, maybe they'd leave. Abe would be heart-broken if the daughter of his old friend was murdered out here. And Jeff wouldn't be with the wagons to try to prevent it. Abe would never forgive him for that.

A dozen possibilities of what could have happened were muddling his thinking when at last he saw the white canvas of a wagon top in the light of the late rising moon. He was sure that he wasn't far from the water hole at Cheyenne Wells on the headwaters of the south fork of the Smoky Hill River. If so, what had happened? Why hadn't Beany brought the wagons farther during the day?

A possible answer hit him and he reined up. Maybe

Terpko and Ivie had captured the wagons and had halted them, preparing to catch Jeff in a trap when he returned. If the whole thing had been a trap as he was guessing, what better way to spring it than to wait for Jeff to ride into camp?

Reining off the road, Jeff slowly circled the wagons. Nothing appeared amiss but there wasn't enough light to see any details. He'd wait till morning. If Terpko and Ivie were not here and came in during the night, he'd know it and take a hand. If they were already at the wagons, he'd only get himself killed by riding in blindly now.

Dismounting behind a knoll, he loosened the cinch on his horse and let him crop grass while Jeff kept a watch on the white topped wagons. Nothing stirred and Jeff began to feel foolish lying out here within sight of camp but afraid to ride in.

Dawn came at last. Still nothing stirred around the wagons. Jeff concluded that either no one was there or else Terpko and Ivie had the camp under control and were keeping everyone out of sight until they got the chance to kill Jeff as he rode into the camp.

Fretting with uneasiness, Jeff waited. If it was a trap, surely some movement around the camp would give it away. If the two men had taken everyone away from the wagons, Jeff had to find out soon so he could get on their trail.

As the light strengthened, he assured himself that they were still there because he could see the horses. Even Angel, Beany's mule, was there. Then Samson came out from under a wagon, stretched, and trotted around the wagons. He carefully avoided the area behind the rear wagon where the goats were. If the people were gone, Samson would not be here. But where was everyone?

Jeff held his taut nerves in check. Something would have to give soon. The captors of the wagons apparently wanted Jeff to think the wagons were deserted. But they must have forgotten about the animals, especially Samson. No dog would act as Samson did if his master was not there.

Then Beany climbed out of the front wagon, saying something over his shoulder to someone behind him. He began gathering buffalo chips for a fire. Jeff hoped he would come close enough that he could attract his attention. But this was not a regular campsite and chips were plentiful within a few yards of the wagons.

Bessie came out of the middle wagon when Beany had the fire going and began breakfast. There was no sign of Norrie or any of the girls. The fact that Beany and Bessie came out of the wagons was a give-away. In this hot weather, they wouldn't sleep in the wagons. Beany and Norrie hadn't slept in the wagons since leaving Kansas City except for one night when it rained. It hadn't rained last night.

Jeff couldn't think of any way to attract Beany's attention. As he lay there trying to think of some way to get word to Beany, the girls climbed out of the wagon. The last one out of the middle wagon was Posey and Ivie was right behind her. Even from this distance, Jeff could see he had a grip on her arm and one hand behind her back. There was probably a gun in that hand. His eyes swept the prairies to the west and south and north. Jeff kept his head low.

Looking again, he noticed that Cheery wasn't with the girls. Then Norrie climbed out of the front wagon followed by Cheery and Terpko. Terpko was holding Cheery the same way Ivie was holding Posey.

Jeff fumed. If the two men would get away from the girls, he would be tempted to try his skill as marksman. They were likely aware of that and they obviously expected him to be here now.

About the time Bessie called them to breakfast, Jeff got an idea. It was a far-fetched one but it might work. Crawling back down the knoll out of sight of the camp, he dug in his pockets for a piece of paper and a stub pencil, two items he always carried when he was guiding a wagon train. He often had to write out instructions while he went ahead to scout. Now he wrote a note to Beany.

The note was simple. It told Beany to pass the word to Norrie and the girls to start a disturbance. Jeff would try to take advantage of it.

His problem now was to get that note to Beany. His eye was on Samson but the dog was waiting patiently as the people ate breakfast, hoping to get some scraps. Jeff noted that everyone seemed to be all right. He imagined Posey looked beaten up but he couldn't be sure from this distance.

After making sure everyone was busy with breakfast, Jeff slid back out of sight of the camp. Throwing back his head, he howled, imitating the yap-yap-yow-w-w-ow of a coyote as best he could. He doubted if it was a good imitation but both Terpko and Ivie were city men. They weren't likely to detect the false notes. Beany would and Jeff was banking on that.

He was also banking on Samson responding to the howl. He wasn't disappointed in that. Jeff lifted his head just enough to peek over. Samson had forgotten about breakfast and was staring out at the knoll behind which Jeff was hidden. He was curious but not enough to leave the intriguing smell of breakfast.

Jeff backed down the knoll and repeated the howl. Inching his way up to the top agian, he stared over. The entire camp was looking his way now. Terpko and Ivie were on the alert. But Beany shrugged and turned back to his plate, saying something that seemed to ease the tension. Samson came out a ways from the camp and barked.

Jeff slid back and repeated the howl. Samson barked louder and came closer. Jeff howled again. Samson, apparently not believing that it was a coyote, something he had learned from bitter experience to stay away from, came almost to the top of the knoll.

Jeff inched up to the top of the knoll again. Those at the fire were eating again but looking at the top of the hill once in a while. Samson was just on the other side and Jeff spoke softly to him. Samson's bristles dropped immediately and he came over the hill, wagging his tail. Jeff wondered if those in camp had noticed the change in the dog.

He patted Samson then quickly slipped the note he had written under the collar of the dog. Beany kept a collar on him in case he wanted to tie him up which he did once in a while when prairie wolves howled close by.

"Go on back," Jeff ordered. When the dog just stood there, Jeff repeated the order in a sharp tone. Samson ducked his head in bewilderment at Jeff's scolding but didn't leave until Jeff had repeated the order again, sharper than ever.

The dog went back over the knoll and trotted toward camp. Jeff crawled to the top to watch. Beany had obviously recognized the false note in the coyote howl and had been watching Samson. Now he came to the edge of camp to meet him. He reached down to pet him. Jeff couldn't be sure that he found the note before Terpko yelled at him and he wheeled obediently and went back to the fire and his breakfast plate.

All Jeff could do now was wait. He had the rifle off his saddle and was waiting for a break. When Posey had turned toward the fire once, he got a look at the little gun the gambler had in his hand. Jeff was sure Terpko had a gun, too. It was a touchy situation. If Jeff used the rifle, he'd have to make sure his aim was good and he'd have to be fast to get both men before one of them killed someone in camp. It was just too big a risk.

Beany moved around, helping clear up the breakfast plates. There was no move being made to start the wagons. Jeff squirmed as the sun grew hotter. Had Beany gotten his message? Even if he had, what could he do?

Ivie retreated to the middle wagon with Posey while Terpko backed off to squat down by the hub of the front wagon. He still kept Cheery in front of him and

Ivie kept this gun on Posey. It looked like a stalemate.

Then Toni sat down not far from the fire and crossed her legs. Jeff recognized the signs. She had done that back at Big Timbers when she had pretended to go into a trance and Terpko had been scared into confessing his part in the scheme to keep Jeff from getting to Abe's ranch. Toni must be going to do her act again.

When she began rocking slowly back and forth, Jeff knew he was right. He couldn't hear what she was saying but he heard Terpko yell for her to stop it. Bessie suddenly jumped back as if startled by something, spilling the warm dishwater on the ground, splashing it toward Terpko.

Just as Terpko yelled at Bessie Lily began singing in a high shrill voice. Ivie prodded Posey out from the wagon, his eyes sweeping everyone as if he expected one of them to pull a gun on him. Terpko shook a fist.

"Shut up, everybody!" he yelled.

Nobody paid any attention to him. Jeff fingered his rifle nervously, wondering if he could get a bead on Terpko in case he decided to shut somebody up with his gun. Beany had moved away from the fire, Jeff noticed, and was now at the head of his mule, Angel.

Suddenly Angel began braying. Jeff didn't know what Beany was doing but it was something that irritated the mule. Hercules came around from the back of the wagons to see what was going on.

Terpko was close to the fire now, his gun still on Cheery. Suddenly he turned the gun on Star. "Get over here," he yelled loud enough for Jeff to hear, his eye on the goat. "If you don't come, I'll shoot that goat."

Star came. It was the one threat that would make her obey almost any command. Terpko had seen what Hercules could do when he got roused and he apparently planned to forestall that by holding Star at the point of his gun.

"Now everybody quiet down," Terpko yelled. "Somebody better explain what all the fuss is about or you're going to be sorry."

"Toni sees trouble for the strangers in camp," Bessie said loud enough for Jeff to hear. "We are just trying to ward off the evil spirits."

"There ain't no such thing as evil spirits," Ivie shouted. "Terpko, you get that goat away from here."

"That's Star's job," Terpko said. "She knows I'll kill him if he starts anything."

The mule brayed again. Jeff could see that Beany was teasing Angel and the mule was mad, jerking back on his rope.

"Get away from that mule," Terpko yelled. "Get over here with the others."

Beany came but he left an angry mule behind him. Bessie hovered over Toni. Suddenly she straightened and started slowly toward Terpko as if hypnotized. Lily was still singing shrilly. Jeff would have grinned at the confusion they were creating if it hadn't been so serious.

Terpko was watching Bessie and now he shouted at her to get back. Ivie had moved Posey out near the fire. He yelled for everybody to quiet down or he'd start shooting. Jeff sighted his rifle on Ivie, considering him more dangerous than Terpko.

Nobody paid any attention to the shouts of either man. Bessie moved closer to Terpko and Star. Star didn't move even when Terpko nudged her with his gun.

"Get back, you old hag!" Terpko yelled. "I'll shoot."

"The spirit says you're going to die," Bessie yelled and Jeff could detect the fury in her voice all the way up on the knoll. "You'll see who is an old hag."

"Don't come any closer!" Terpko warned. It was obvious he was afraid of Bessie and, considering the mood she was in now, Jeff didn't blame him.

"You've got only one chance to live," Bessie said, keeping a steady advance on Terpko. "Leave this place at once."

"I ain't going nowhere," Terpko shouted. "You stop or I'll shoot!"

Bessie moved closer and suddenly Terpko pointed his gun in the air and fired. Bessie stopped. Evidently she hadn't thought he would go that far. Toni stopped rocking back and forth but she didn't get up. Lily's song was cut off in the middle of a high note.

Terpko had succeeded in stopping the disturbance. But he had created some he hadn't expected. All the train's horses were staked outside the camp. Only Terpko's and Ivie's horses were in camp and they were saddled and tied to wagon wheels.

They had evidently caught some of the excitement that Angel's braying had generated. Both horses jerked back on their reins. One broke loose and thundered out of camp.

Terpko's nerves broke and he lunged for the horse as

it raced past him. Star immediately dodged away from him. Hercules saw Terpko running his way and shook his head angrily. Terpko saw the goat and stopped so fast, his boots slid on the grass. Then he wheeled toward the one horse that was still tied.

Ivie yelled at Terpko but Terpko ignored him. Seeing he was going to be left alone, Ivie dashed for the horse, too. Terpko beat him to the animal and jerked the reins loose, swinging into the saddle. Before Ivie could reach him, Terpko was thundering out of camp.

Ivie wheeled around, panic finally hitting him. Jeff had his sights on the gambler but as long as he didn't threaten to shoot anyone, he'd let the panic run its course.

The only animal left near the wagons was Angel and Ivie made a dash for the mule.

"Not my mule!" Beany roared but Jeff could tell there was no anger in his words.

Ivie wheeled on Beany and swung up his gun. Jeff pulled the trigger on the rifle, sending the shot over the camp. That was the last straw for Ivie. He lunged toward the mule, panic in complete control.

As Ivie approached the mule, Angel wheeled and kicked at him. He was a one man mule, anyway, and right now he was still raging from the teasing Beany had given him.

Ivie ran to Angel's side and reached for him. Angel wheeled and doubled up, getting his feet against Ivie as he kicked, sending him rolling. Hercules, seeing all the action that he was missing, bleated and ran toward Ivie. Ivie saw him and scrambled to his feet and made another dive at Angel. This time Angel's hoofs caught Ivie as he was coming in. The little gambler was lifted off his feet and sent in a shapeless heap several feet away. Even Hercules didn't bother to charge him after he landed.

Jeff was on his feet and running toward the camp. That last kick from Angel had hit Ivie in the chest. He wasn't going to be bothering anyone for a few minutes. Jeff intended to be there when he came to.

Reaching the camp, he knelt beside Beany near Ivie. It took only one look at the cave-in chest to tell Jeff that Ivie wasn't going to bother anybody for a long time if ever again.

"You said to create a disturbance," Beany said. "I didn't expect to kill anybody."

"You didn't," Jeff said. "If he dies, he got just what all horse and mule thieves usually get. Only he got it first hand." He looked around. "Everybody all right?"

"All except me," Bessie said. "I was cheated. I wanted to get my hands on Terpko. He'd have found out how hard an old hag can squeeze. I'd have made him look like a starved snake."

Jeff wished, too, that they had caught Terpko. He could still cause trouble.

XVI

"Can we do anything for him?" Toni asked softly, looking down at Ivie.

"He's still breathing," Jeff said, putting a hand on his smashed chest. "Don't know for how long, though."

Ivie opened his eyes, the pain showing clearly in them. His lips moved and Jeff leaned closer to listen.

"Weight on my chest," Ivie whispered. "Get it off.

"I'm afraid I can't," Jeff said. "The mule kicked you. Where will Terpko go?"

Realization of death was in Ivie's eyes. "To the AR," he said after a moment. "Grilli and—Terpko will get—everything. My share—"

Another question came to Jeff's lips but he didn't put it into words. It was too late. Ivie wouldn't answer any more questions. Jeff got slowly to his feet. He'd had no love for Ivie; not even any respect; but it still was not a pretty sight to see a man die like that.

"We ain't more than a few miles from the bluff where we buried Zorn," Beany said softly. "Should we take him back?"

Jeff thought for a moment. "It won't make any difference to him now where he's buried. And it may make a lot of difference to Uncle Abe how quick we can get to the AR."

"Reckon that's right," Beany said. "Come on, Norrie. Let's dig a hole."

The three men cut a rectangle in the grass and began

digging out the dirt underneath. Jeff took his turn and while he was resting, Posey came over to him.

"They were after the money," she said.

Jeff nodded. "I figured as much. I thought he'd be after you, too. He struck me as a man who would get revenge if he thought he had it coming to him."

"He intended to kill me," Posey said. "He threatened to a half dozen times but he wanted that money and I wouldn't tell him where it was. If I'd told him, he'd have killed me and left."

"He'd have killed everybody else first so nobody would have been alive to tell who killed you. Did he give you that black eye and that bruise on your face?"

Posey nodded. "I wasn't going to tell him, no matter what. Only part of that money belonged to his brother, anyway, and I imagine Bud either stole that or cheated someone out of it."

"By stalling, you gave me time to get here," Jeff said. "And you saved Uncle Abe's money, too."

Jeff took his turn digging again. When the work was done and Ivie had been buried as decently as time and circumstances would allow, Jeff called for the wagons to get ready to move again. However, it was nearing noon before the wagons actually began rolling.

Jeff moved out ahead, impatient at the delay. Every minute he was held back gave Grilli that much more time to perform his mischief. Jeff considered the possibility that Grilli would murder Abe and his wife, Miranda. Although he couldn't quite believe that of Grilli, he did expect him to try something to bring him a lot of money. If Abe got in the way, then Grilli might kill him. And Abe would get in the way if he discovered Grilli was out to rob him. Jeff had to get to the AR as quickly as possible.

They were far out on the dry divide between the Smoky Hill River and Big Sandy Creek when Jeff spotted riders ahead. He shaded his eyes against the afternoon sun but he couldn't identify them against the light.

Reining up, he eased his gun free in its holster and pulled his rifle from its boot, laying it across his thighs. There were three riders so that ruled out Terpko and Grilli unless they had another henchman with them. Jeff waited, tense and uneasy.

Then one of the riders raised an arm and shouted. Jeff recognized Johnny Boe, the oldest hand, next to Beany, on Abe's ranch. Jeff would guess Johnny to be about thirty.

Touching his horse with his spurs, he trotted forward. There were two AR cowboys with Johnny. Jeff recognized Ding Peddiwell, the little hand that Abe said had to stand twice to make a shadow. He wasn't much over five feet tall. The other rider was a man Jeff hadn't seen before. Likely a man that Abe had hired since Jeff had been on the AR.

"Glad we ran into you," Johnny said as he reached out a hand to Jeff. "You know Ding here. This other hombre is Ed Walling. We're looking for a stray herd of steers."

Jeff shook hands with the other two men then turned a frown on Johnny. "A stray herd? Stolen?"

Johnny nodded grimly. "That's it. We were taking a

big herd of AR steers to Deer Trail to ship them when Ross Gossy came back from somewhere and he had a half dozen tough hands with him. They got the drop on us and just took over and headed the herd southeast. We figured they was heading for Kit Carson to ship them out but nobody there had seen the herd."

"Maybe they turned north to Cheyenne," Jeff suggested.

Boe shook his head. "I don't think so. We trailed them down past the Big Bend of the Sandy and then they seemed to angle south away from the river. There ain't no place down there where they can ship those critters so we figured they'd swing in to Kit Carson. We hoped to catch them there."

"Maybe you got there ahead of them," Jeff said.

"Maybe. And maybe they decided to go on to Kansas, possibly Sheridan. They could claim they came from Texas or even western Kansas. Abe's brand might be recognized in Kit Carson but not in Kansas."

"That makes sense," Jeff admitted. "But most buyers don't pay a lot of attention to brands, anyway. Getting the critters in their possession is all they want. If you boys spread out to the north and south, you should cut the trail of the herd if it went east."

"Sort of what we figured," Boe said. He grinned. "How about giving us a peek at your cargo?"

"The girls? I thought you had better sense than to let Beany pick a wife for you, Johnny."

"Hold on," Johnny said. "I didn't promise to marry what Beany brought back. But he ain't no slouch at picking the pretty ones at dances. We figured he'd do all right in Kansas City. Besides, we had to agree to the deal or Abe was going to fire the whole kit and kaboodle of us."

"He must have been pretty riled up," Jeff said.

"Sort of. All of us but Beany had been to Denver and we were three days late getting back. That's when Abe blew his cork and sent Beany to Kansas City for the girls. He thinks we'll settle down if we're hitched."

"Glad I'm just bringing them to you, not marrying them," Jeff said.

Boe looked sharply at Jeff. "Didn't Beany tell you? You're to get one of them, too."

"Me?" Jeff exploded. "That old reprobate! Beany never mentioned that. Just that Abe had a job for me when I got to the AR."

"He has," Johnny said. "He ain't able to get around and run things like he used to. You'll get that job. Maybe he'll even give you the foreman job instead of me. Now how about looking at the girls?"

"Why not?" Jeff said. "I reckon they're as anxious to look at you boys as you are to see them."

"Got a little short one for me?" Ding asked.

"Maybe," Jeff said. It seemed to him that all the girls were taller than Ding. But he knew that Toni was shorter. She was just about an even five feet. Ding was a little taller than that. Jeff frowned. Ding wasn't right for Toni. Neither was Johnny; nor the new hand, Ed Walling.

Wheeling his horse, he started back toward the wagons, which had moved closer while he talked with

174

Johnny Boe. Beany came from the wagons on his mule and greeted the three AR hands.

"Which one is for me?" Johnny asked as they neared the wagons, which had stopped. The girls popped out of the middle wagon to stand in a line, looking the cowboys over. Jeff wondered if Beany had recognized the AR hands and had told the girls these were the men they had come to marry.

"You do your own picking," Beany said. "And no fights, ding-bust it, or I'll knock off some heads."

Jeff, looking at the girls, suddenly realized that what Johnny had said was likely true. There were five girls and there were only four AR hands, counting Ross Grilli. Beany would never consent to marrying one of them. So that extra girl was for Jeff. Well, Abe could just go sit on a cactus. Nobody was going to tell *him* when he was going to get married!

With Grilli turned outlaw, Abe really needed only three girls to tie down all his crew in matrimony. But as he thought of it, he decided that Posey would likely go on to Denver where she could quickly get into business again. There would still be one extra.

Jeff left the job of introducing the girls and the AR hands to Beany. After all, Abe had put him in charge of this project. Bessie stood in front of the girls and sized up the men as they dismounted and advanced, hats in their hands.

"I've seen worse," Bessie concluded, looking each man over carefully. "But I've seen better, too."

"You've seen better days, too, if anybody asks," Beany said sharply.

"Nobody asking you," Bessie retorted. "Your good days are so far behind you, it would take the memory of an elephant to recall them."

Jeff decided on this spot for the night camp. His urgency to get to the AR was gone now that Boe had told him Grilli had stolen the AR herd and was trailing them across the prairie somewhere. At least, Abe wasn't in any immediate danger.

While Bessie and the girls began supper, Jeff made a suggestion to Johnny Boe. "At dawn, we'll spread out, two of us go south of the trail and two north. If Grilli has moved the herd east, we'll cut the trail somewhere."

Boe nodded but his eyes were on the girls. Jeff guessed that Abe hadn't had such a hard time in convincing his hands that Beany could pick good wives for them. It surprised him. Most cowboys wanted girls, all right, but not wives. He didn't see any reluctance on the part of the three AR riders to tie the knot.

Hercules came around to inspect the visitors and Beany issued a warning. "Watch that four-legged son of Satan, Johnny. He'll butt anything he can reach with that brainless head of his."

Johnny reached out a hand and rubbed the goat between the eyes. Hercules shook his head but didn't back off nor did he threaten to charge. Jeff watched in surprise. Johnny Boe was about the first person, other than Star, that Hercules would allow to touch him.

"He's a pretty goat," Johnny said.

"About as pretty as the gates of Purgatory," Beany muttered.

Star noticed Johnny patting the goat and came over, ostensibly to claim the goat. But she didn't call the goat away. She began talking to Johnny. Within a minute, the goat was being ignored by both of them.

"Who'd have thought it?" Beany muttered to Jeff after Jeff had moved away from the two. "The widow with the boy and the plague-taken goats is going to be the first one to snag a man."

"Looks that way," Jeff said. "Let's get ready for an early start tomorrow. You'll take charge of the wagons. I'll help Johnny and the boys try to cut Grilli's trail."

Jeff watched the other two cowboys eyeing the girls after supper. Ding Peddiwell talked with Toni a while. She was the only girl shorter than he was. Jeff squirmed uneasily while they were talking. But Ding didn't stay long. When he moved away, Ed Walling slid over next to Toni. She was the prettiest girl in the bunch, Jeff admitted, but that didn't mean that the new AR hand could just snatch her up like that.

Jeff left his bedroll where he'd been sitting and strolled over close to Walling and Toni.

"Better hit the sack, cowboy," Jeff said. "We've got a lot of riding to do tomorrow."

Walling looked up. "Johnny's the boss of our outfit."

"Johnny's got other things on his mind right now. If Johnny wants to ride sleepy tomorrow, that's his business. But somebody has to be sharp-eyed."

Walling frowned but he got to his feet and, saying something softly to Toni, moved away. Jeff watched him go.

"That really wasn't very nice, was it?" Toni asked Jeff when Walling was gone.

"Wasn't thinking about how nice it was," Jeff said.

Toni smiled. "You're not jealous, are you?"

Jeff frowned at Toni. "Don't let any of them push you into making a quick decision."

"Oh, I won't," Toni said. "Nobody's pushing me."

"Would you look at that?" Beany said when Jeff returned to his blankets. "The long and the short of it."

Jeff looked where Beany was pointing. Out at the edge of the shadows beyond the campfire Lily and Ding were sitting on the ground talking as though they were long lost cousins. She was almost a foot taller than Ding.

Jeff had breakfast early the next morning. He left Beany in charge of the wagons, telling him to move them on toward Kit Carson when they were ready to go. There would be good water there. Johnny Boe and Ding Peddiwell rode to the south while Jeff and Ed Walling went north. They rode back and forth across the prairie, a mile or two apart, looking for any sign of a passing herd.

It was night when they caught up with the wagons. Beany had not hurried the train. They had plenty of water along and they were within half a day of Kit Carson now. Beany didn't want to get too far ahead of the men.

Jeff and Johnny reported to each other. No sign of a herd passing close to the trail. They could have swung far to the south or north but it wasn't likely they could have done that and gotten this far. Tomorrow they would look again.

Beany again.

Ed Walling and Posey paired off that evening, sitting on the tongue of a wagon that was propped up on its neckyoke. Jeff nudged Beany. "What kind of a fellow is Walling?"

Beany shrugged. "A good hand. But he's not the kind to be scared off by a girl like Posey. I told him about her. He's no angel himself. They'd make a good pair. You know, out here away from the kind of life she's had, I sort of like Posey."

Jeff nodded and let the subject drop. He had noticed that the last two evenings, Norrie had ridden close herd on Cheery as if to keep her away from the cowboys. Norrie and Cheery were both young but Jeff found it amusing the way Norrie was establishing his claim on Cheery without saying a word to anyone, least of all Cheery. But she knew. If Norrie thought she didn't, he had a lot to learn about women.

They reached Kit Carson at noon the next day. Jeff and the others had ridden far out on the prairie without seeing any trail of a passing herd.

After dinner, Jeff inquired at the stockyards to see if a herd had come in recently. He was told that there had been none for a week but that a big herd was due in tomorrow for loading the next day.

"That could be our herd," Jeff told Johnny. "We'll ride out to see as soon as it's dark."

Kit Carson was just what was left of an end-of-track town but it had an element of stability about it. The girls and Bessie went into town to look things over and Jeff rode out of camp with Johnny before dark.

They found the herd about five or six miles west of town. Dismounting, they slipped up close enough to identify Ross Grilli at the fire. Johnny said he recognized some of the others. They had been with Grilli when they'd surprised the AR hands and taken the herd.

"I didn't see Terpko," Jeff said as they rode back to camp. "I figured he'd be with them."

"Some of Grilli's men may be in town," Johnny said. "How are we going to stop them from selling those cattle?"

"I'll try to think of a way," Jeff said.

But Jeff's planning was shattered when they rode into camp. There was an uproar at the middle wagon with Bessie bellowing questions at Cheery. Jeff rode over to the wagon and swung down.

"What's wrong?"

Bessie wheeled on him. "Cheery and Toni was behind us coming back from town," she said, her voice shrill, almost a wail. "Hod Terpko surprised them and kidnapped Toni."

XVII

The kick of a mule couldn't have jolted Jeff more than Bessie's news. If Terpko had taken any girl except Toni, it wouldn't have hit him so hard. He had to admit it.

"Why?" he asked, his voice hoarse.

"To make you stand back and let them sell the herd," Cheery said.

"If the sidewinder was going to kidnap someone to make us toe the line, why didn't he take both of them?" Bessie asked.

"Because he wanted Cheery to come back and tell us what happened," Beany said. "What's he going to do with Toni?"

"He said he'd hold her prisoner," Cheery said. "He promised not to hurt her if you don't interfere with their loading the cattle. If you do, he says he'll kill her."

"That ties the knot in the bull's tail," Beany grunted. "We'll have to sit here and watch them sell the cattle and make off with the money."

"Why did he take Toni?" Jeff repeated numbly.

"'Cause he ain't blind," Bessie said. "Neither are any of the rest of us unless it's you. Toni set her cap for you the first time she saw you. And she's had you trapped in it for the last two weeks. Terpko knows he can make you dance to any tune as long as Toni's safety is at stake."

Jeff turned away. Bessie was right. He would do anything to keep Terpko from hurting Toni. But he couldn't let Abe's herd be sold right under his nose, either. Jeff thought of a half dozen schemes that might get the herd away from Grilli and his tough hands. But all of them were too risky while Terpko held Toni.

Jeff paced the area near the wagons long after the others had gone to bed. Beany was on guard although there was little to guard against here. No Indians were liable to bother them this close to town. Grilli and Terpko had no reason to bother them. They already had the hostage they wanted.

Beany came back from the front of the wagon where he had been sitting on the tongue. "Better try to get some sleep, Jeff," he said. "We've got a rough day ahead of us, no matter what we do."

"I don't sleep any until I decide what we can do. There has to be some way to stop them without risking Toni's life."

Johnny Boe came from his blankets. "I ain't much of a sleeper when I've got this much on my mind. Thought of anything yet, Jeff?"

Jeff nodded. "An idea—but it may be too risky."

"Let's hear it," Johnny said.

"Suppose those cattle are still spooky?"

"Might be," Johnny admitted. "They've been on trail a while but I reckon they've been held pretty much in one place for the last few days. They might be ready to run. A stampede would delay them a while."

"If we simply try to stop Grilli's outfit, they'll hurt Toni. Maybe kill her. But if the herd should suddenly

182

stampede, they might not have time to think about Toni." Jeff shook his head. "The risk is pretty big. But I can't think of anything else."

"How do you figure on stampeding that herd without giving Grilli any warning?"

"I'm still mulling it over," Jeff said. "We'll have to move our camp to that swale just about a mile this side of the herd. Remember it, Johnny?"

Johnny Boe nodded. "I recall it. But finding a camp in the trail ain't going to stampede them critters."

"Let's move the wagons," Jeff said. "I'll keep thinking."

The camp was awake in a minute when Jeff passed the word around. It seemed that no one was asleep. The teams were quickly hitched up and the wagons moved out to the west with as little noise as possible. Jeff doubted if the town was even aware of the camp being moved.

Jeff rode far ahead of the wagons, stopping frequently to listen. He reached the swale and rode up the slope to peer over. The moon wasn't up yet. The night was too dark to see much but he knew the herd was down there, less than a mile away.

The thing he had to be wary of now was that the sound of the wagons might carry to the guards watching the herd. He listened but he didn't hear the wagons. The breeze was blowing from the herd toward the wagons, carrying the sound away from the night guards.

When the white topped wagons came in sight in the starlight, Jeff rode back down the slope and met them in the swale. Quietly giving orders, he started the men to unhitching the teams.

"Keep the horses harnessed," he said softly. "Tie them to the backs of the wagons. Stake out those goats. I don't want them tied to the wagons in the morning."

"What have you got in mind?" Beany asked.

"Maybe nothing," Jeff said. "We'll see how things look when it gets light."

The moon came up, only a sliver of its former self. He knew that dawn couldn't be far away. He rode back up the slope, dismounting a short distance from the top. Then he crawled up where he could see over and wasn't likely to be seen when it got light.

As the gray streaks of dawn ran up the eastern sky, the herd became visible down to the west. Two men were riding quietly around the cattle. The chuckwagon was off to the north of the herd. Jeff strained his eyes but couldn't see anything that looked like a prisoner. Likely Toni was in the chuck wagon, he thought. That was about the only place where they could keep her out of sight and still have her with them as they drove the herd to the loading pens.

Jeff didn't move as the light strengthened and the cook climbed out of the wagon and began his fire. The cowboys stirred and when breakfast was ready, one of the men took a tin plate to the front of the cook wagon and handed it to somebody inside. Jeff guessed it was Terpko. Jeff was sure now that Toni was inside that wagon.

Slipping back to his horse, he rode to the wagons. "Hitch up as quiet as you can," he said. "Then bring the wagons up behind the spot where I'll leave my horse."

"Then what?" Beany asked eagerly.

"I'll watch from the top of the hill. When they start the herd, we'll strike if it looks like we can surprise them so much they won't have time to hurt Toni. Tie every coat and rag you have to the tops of the wagons. Then bring those wagons over the hill with the horses on the dead run. Make every bit of noise you can."

Beany grinned. "That should scare the kinks out of those critters. We'll unload anything that can't take that kind of a ride."

While Beany saw to the preparation of the wagons, Jeff went back up the hill, leaving his horses below the level of the hilltop again.

Down at the camp, breakfast was over. The cattle had been up and grazing since dawn. Now the foreman motioned for his men to start the herd moving. The chuckwagon was hitched up and it started toward town, keeping well to the north of the herd. That was just the way Jeff wanted it.

When all the men were working with the herd, Jeff motioned to the drivers of the wagon to get ready. Beany had taken over one wagon, Norrie was holding the reins in his wagon, but Bessie refused to let Johnny Boe or any of the AR cowboys handle the reins on her wagon.

Jeff was amazed at the stringers, coats, petticoats, and dresses that were tied to the tops of the canvas-covered arches. When those wagons began rolling and the breeze hit those banners, it was going to be a sight to frighten minds a lot more stable than the brains of a spooky steer.

Jeff waited until the herd was half way up the knoll. The men on point were just below the crest when Jeff ran back to his horse. With a wave of his hand, he started forward. Behind him, he heard the whips crack and the creak and rumble of the wagons as they accelerated from a standstill to a thundering run. By the time they broke over the top of the hill, the banners tied to the wagons were flapping like wounded eagles.

The drivers began shouting and yelling, Bessie's voice overriding that of all the others. The goats, all three free now because Star wouldn't leave them staked out where they might be run over by a stampede, were keeping up with the charge, Hercules bleating a challenge to any that could hear him. Samson was out in front, barking as if he were within a yard of a plump rabbit. The excitement told him he was after something although he didn't know what.

To the steers, Jeff knew that must make a terrifying sight. The three wagons were coming right out of the sun, reflecting its light, with dresses, petticoats, and rags flapping wildly in the morning breeze. It was enough to make any self-respecting steer reconsider his path in life. And these steers had their full share of self respect.

They stopped dead in their tracks at the first sight of the three ponderous, white-topped, banner-decorated wagons lumbering over the hill at them with all the speed those teams could muster. That sight, coupled with the noise that accompanied it, was too much. With the suddenness of an explosion, the lead steers wheeled and charged away from the apparition, taking with them every critter in the herd.

The two riders on point must have felt as useless as a hair ribbon on a bald head. They wheeled and charged after the herd, showing an uncontrollable affection for those steers that they had never demonstrated before.

Jeff reined his horse to the right, aiming directly toward the chuckwagon. That team, although quite a distance from the charging wagons, had caught the excitement that was spreading over the prairie like a fire and were jerking at the reins in an effort to join the general exodus from the area. The driver was fighting to control the horses.

Jeff had almost reached the wagon when the team jerked free of the driver's restraining grip and started running. Wheeling up even with the horse on the near side, Jeff grabbed a bridle and jerked back, bringing the bit against the horse's mouth and causing him to forget his fright and yield to the pinch of the bit.

In fifty yards, Jeff had the team halted. They were well out of the path of the stampede which was in full flight now. Jeff wheeled on the driver, expecting trouble. But the driver, who was just a boy and was probably the flunkey around camp, seemed more appreciative of having the runaway stopped then he was fearful of the man who had stopped it.

"Where's the girl?" Jeff demanded.

The boy couldn't get the lump out of his throat to make a sound but he jerked his thumb toward the covered part of the wagon.

"Hold those horses," Jeff ordered and leaped into the wagon. He found Toni tied to the side of the wagon box. It took only a minute to get her free.

"Are you all right?" he asked, suddenly finding her in his arms and liking the feel of her closeness.

"Scared, that's all," she said.

He pulled away from her and jumped out of the wagon, reaching up to help her down. He heard hoofbeats and wheeled to see Beany coming up on Angel.

"Grilli broke away and I tried chasing him," Beany panted, pulling up the mule. "Angel just ain't cut out for racing. I'll take care of Toni if you'll go after that sidewinder. He's the ring leader."

Jeff was already running for his horse. "Seen Terpko? I've got a score to settle with him, too."

"Can't tell what is going on in all that dust and running," Beany said. "I just happened to recognize Grilli when he turned yellow and headed for safer pastures."

Jeff hit the saddle and wheeled his horse. A rider was just disappearing over the ridge to the north of the stampede. It would be like Ross Grilli to run if things were going bad for him. And there was little doubt that things were going very bad for the rustlers now. The stampede was in full flight to the west. It would take a long while to round up the steers, even if the rustlers could overpower the AR cowboys, which was doubtful in all this confusion. Grilli apparently felt that escape from a sinking venture was the best policy.

It was a hard chase and Jeff wasn't sure for a while whether he could catch Grilli. But Grilli, aware that he was being chased, turned frequently to look back. It was during one of these backward looks that he pulled too hard on the reins and jerked his horse's head around so far that he couldn't see the drop-off into a gully. The horse fell, throwing Grilli over his head into the opposite bank of the gully.

Jeff kicked his horse into a greater effort, recognizing his momentary advantage. Grilli was just staggering to his feet, still dazed, when Jeff arrived. Grilli saw him and clawed for his gun but Jeff left his saddle in a long dive, driving his shoulder into Grilli's stomach. The air exploded from Grilli and the fight went out of him with equal suddenness.

Jeff jerked the gun out of Grilli's hand and tossed it away then pulled him to his feet. His fury was at its peak but there was no satisfaction in beating something that wouldn't fight back.

"I've come a long way to get my horse and my money and to make a few dents in your skull," Jeff panted. "Are you going to fight?"

Grilli just stared at him, not lifting a hand to defend himself.

"Get on your horse," Jeff said disgustedly. "I'll let Uncle Abe settle with you."

The cattle had stopped running when Jeff got Grilli back in sight of the herd but they were scattered over a thousand acres. Jeff found Beany and Johnny Boe together.

"Thought you'd get him," Beany said, his face creased in satisfaction. "You always claimed to be a ring-tailed tiger," he said to Grilli. "What happened?

Get that tail in a crack?"

Grilli didn't answer. Jeff looked at the scattered cattle. "How long will it take to round up those critters?"

"A couple of days," Johnny said. "The rest of Grilli's crew headed for empty country like scalded ghosts."

"All except Terpko," Beany added. "He got tangled up with a passel of hoofs and horns. We found what was left of him right in the middle of what had been the stampede."

"Where's Toni?"

"I wondered when you'd get around to that," Beany said, grinning. "She's with the other girls at the wagons. Johnny sent Ding to Kit Carson to send a message to Abe who should be waiting for word from us at Deer Trail. He'll come down on the train and will be here when we ship the cattle out."

"You'd better get started rounding them up or they'll be half way back to the ranch."

"Figured on that," Beany said. "We'll take care of Grilli. As soon as you get through mooning over Toni, you can come out and help us with the cattle."

Jeff wheeled his horse and rode to the wagons. The girls were untying the rags and clothes from the bows of the wagons. Toni saw him coming and hopped down and ran to meet him. He reined up and swung off his horse. He reached for her and she came to him willingly. Then she suddenly pushed back.

"Wait a minute! I promised to marry a cowboy when I got out here."

He frowned. "Well, if I don't qualify, there's Johnny,

and Ding, and Ed. Why don't you marry one of them?"

"None of them have asked me?"

He saw the twinkle in her eyes; she was baiting him. "I'm no good with words," he said. "I'll do my asking like this."

He pulled her to him and gave her a kiss like he'd been dreaming of doing half way across Kansas. When he released her, she stepped back and took a deep breath.

"That was some question," she said.

"What's the answer?"

She gave him as good as he had given her. She left no doubt as to her answer.

Center Point Publishing
600 Brooks Road ● PO Box 1
Thorndike ME 04986-0001 USA

(207) 568-3717

**US & Canada:
1 800 929-9108**